The Inevitable Hunt

STAND-ALONE NOVEL

A Western Historical Adventure Book

by

Zachary McCrae

Disclaimer & Copyright

This is a work of fiction. Names, characters, places and incidents either are products of the author's imagination or are used fictitiously. Any resemblance to actual events or locales or persons, living or dead, is entirely coincidental.

Table of Contents

The Inevitable Hunt 1

   Disclaimer & Copyright 2

   Table of Contents 3

   Letter from Zachary McCrae 5

Prologue 6

Chapter One 11

Chapter Two 17

Chapter Three 23

Chapter Four 30

Chapter Five 38

Chapter Six 45

Chapter Seven 52

Chapter Eight 59

Chapter Nine 68

Chapter Ten 72

Chapter Eleven 77

Chapter Twelve 83

Chapter Thirteen 88

Chapter Fourteen 93

Chapter Fifteen 98

Chapter Sixteen 103

Chapter Seventeen 108

Chapter Eighteen 114

Chapter Nineteen 123

Chapter Twenty 130

Chapter Twenty-one..134

Chapter Twenty-two..141

Epilogue 145

Extended Epilogue..148

Also by Zachary McCrae..151

Letter from Zachary McCrae

I'm a man who loves plain things; a cup of strong coffee in the morning, a good book at noon and his wife's embrace at night. I want to write stories that take you from the hand and show you what it meant to be someone who tried to make ends meet and find their own way in 19-century United States. I've been this someone for a long time in my life, always looking for my next gig after my parents' sudden death, always finding new friends but somehow not being able to stick with 'em. It's easy to find quantity in your life but what about quality?

At the age of 50, and after my baby boy, Jeb, and my sweet daughter, Janette, went away to study East, with my sweet wife, Mrs. Maryanne Mc Crae, we moved back to my home town and my dad's ranch close to the Rockies. After a series of health issues that have brought me even closer to our Lord, I've officially started writing those stories I always loved to read. I'm tending my land and animals now with the help of Maryanne, and I'm grateful for each day I get to walk on this world we call earth. As the saying goes, "Nature gave us all something to fall back on, and sooner or later we all land flat on it," so I want to take care of it just the way it has taken care of my dad and mom, and my cousins.

My adventure stories are my legacy to my children and to all of the readers that will honor me by following my work. God bless you and your families and our land! Thank you.

Stay safe but adventurous,

Zachary McCrae

Prologue

Amarillo, Texas 1881

When Aaron burst into the office, Jeb Barnett knew whatever was coming wasn't going to be good. Jeb had seen his fair share of ugly situations, and not only since pinning on the sheriff's star. Life in Amarillo in 1881 wasn't exactly a cakewalk, but something that could get Aaron's usually calm demeanor out of sorts was something Jeb wasn't looking forward to hearing about. Jeb set aside some paperwork and looked up at the man. The blond hair and blue eyes gave Aaron a younger look, in contrast with Jeb's dark hair and eyes. Most wouldn't have guessed, but they'd grown up together in the town.

The small, worn-down station where they sat had been there since as long as either could remember. The office in front had only room for a desk and two chairs, the majority of the building being taken up by cells off a hallway to the back.

"It's Richard," was all the man had to say before Jeb was up and grabbing his hat from a peg on the wall.

Richard Tulley was one of Jeb's most trusted deputies. Alongside Aaron, the trio had made big moves to clean up the Texas county over the years. It had made them some enemies, sure, but the majority of the people were on their side, happy and thankful to know the streets they walked were a little safer each day thanks to the lawmen. Naturally, threats had been made, words had been exchanged. Jeb knew when he traded his days running the ranch for keeping order he was also trading the peace of days out on the range. Until now, at least, things had never gotten too close to home. They had in the past. It was what drew him to the job. But, Jeb had no intention of letting anyone else suffer what he had. Aaron's expression made him think he was perhaps too late. Again.

***

Aaron had described the scene as the men rode out to Richard's homestead, but words never seemed to truly paint the picture one was walking into in a situation like this. Thankfully, a neighbor had been in the vicinity and was able to track down Aaron who tended to the family as best he could before riding out to get Jeb. But no amount of preparation could reduce the shock and sickness Jeb felt when he stepped across the threshold and into Richard's home. Out on the edge of town like this, things tended to be quiet. Jeb himself had chosen his home for that very reason. Like most towns, the closer one got to the center, the rowdier things could become. It was the perfect place for the sheriff's station, but in the evening, the lawmen tended to choose calmer, more removed areas to call home.

The general disarray, the overturned table, broken chairs and windows — these things were not uncommon in Jeb's experience. But the setting, seeing this was the table where he'd had many a dinner, seeing these were the chairs and windows Jeb had helped build when Richard moved to town and took the deputy's position, this carried a heavier weight. Richard's body was crumpled in the corner of the room, an arm thrown back across his eyes as if shielding him from the horror of his home.

Richard's children, little four-year-old Benjamin and Daisy, not even six months yet, had come to feel like Jeb's own. Since losing his own family that dark day, Jeb had done his best to keep acquaintances at an arm's length, all relationships professional and attachments loose. But Shae Tulley, Richard's wife — *Widow*, Jeb corrected himself — hadn't tolerated any of Jeb's stand-offishness. The woman who had been nearly as much of a part of their team as any other now sat huddled in the corner, a blanket wrapped around her shoulders covering her just past the knee, Daisy quietly suckling at her breast.

"It was the best I could do," Aaron was saying quietly beside him. "And she fought me on that, too. I don't know who was here, Jeb, but they ransacked this place." He swallowed. "They didn't leave her alone either."

Jeb looked over at the man briefly, understanding the weight of the words, and slowly made his way over to where Shae sat silently, staring off into empty space, the baby in her arms and Benjamin curled up asleep beside her. The woman's long dark hair hung in tangles around her face. Tears had made streaks down her cheeks through the dust and dirt kicked up during the attack. A cut split her bottom lip. He reached out to pull the blanket up slightly higher on her shoulder, but the woman jerked back, fear still overwhelming recognition in her eyes.

Jeb slowly moved his hand back. "It's all right," he whispered. "It's over now. You're safe."

Shae merely pulled Daisy closer to her chest with one arm, putting a protective hand over her sleeping son next to her.

"It's okay," Jeb said again, quietly. He kept his movements slow, deliberate, his open hands out to his sides. Holding the woman's gaze, he backed across the room to where Aaron still stood at the door, gesturing the man outside to the porch.

The wooden overhang that he, Aaron, and Richard had repaired the previous summer was still solid, giving shade and a blessed coolness from the glaring Texas sun. Richard had cut down every tree around the place, Jeb remembered. The former deputy had loved the open view, the city close, but off in the distance just enough to be appreciated without being overwhelming.

"What all do we know?" Jeb asked the deputy.

"Not a lot," Aaron said. "After fetching you I was fixing to head back out and find the neighbor fella that pulled me in. Figured I'd talk to him, have a sit-down with folks out this way. Find out what people seen or heard. Figure out if there's been any new faces in town."

"She say anything to you yet?" Jeb asked.

"Naw," Aaron said. "Don't expect her to, either. She fought me enough about the blanket, but I couldn't just let her lay there exposed."

"I appreciate that," the sheriff said. "I'm sure she will too, eventually. For now, go find out anything you can. Someone comes after one of us like this, I get the feeling it's no accident."

"Want me to send the doc over?"

"Yeah," Jeb said. "Him and his wife, too, if ya can. I think Shae's probably seen enough men for one day."

"You got it, Jeb. Anything else?"

Jeb looked out at the vastness of the territory. He'd been chasing down men for years in the scrub, the dust, the unforgiving heat in this and the surrounding counties. A man could make it real difficult to be found, if he so desired. But, Jeb thought, no one could hide forever. If it took the rest of his days, Jeb was going to find the men responsible for this and bring them to justice.

"Jeb?" Aaron said again, bringing him out of his reverie.

"No," Jeb said, looking over at the man. "You go out and gather up some information. Just don't come back empty-handed."

The deputy looked as if he was going to speak, then instead nodded curtly and walked over to his horse, saddling up and riding off without another word. Jeb watched the dust cloud form behind the man, pondering the best way to let the woman know she would be protected, or what would also be the surest way to find the degenerates responsible. The scene in the home left Jeb with more questions than answers. A struggle, a murder, but no robbery. An attack on the woman, but no clear sign of why.

Something in the back of Jeb's mind taunted him. It should be clearer than this. His only theory so far though, that Richard was targeted specifically because he was a lawman, was something Jeb knew could be the beginning of something dangerous for everyone in the town, not just the ones with stars.

Chapter One

Later that evening, Shae sat at the smooth wooden dining table in the sheriff's home. The sun had set on the day; her children were sleeping upstairs in an extra room, but unless it came from pure exhaustion, Shae didn't see any sleep in her near future. Every time she closed her eyes, horror came to her vision. The violence. The blood. The screams. Poor Richard, gunned down simply for wanting to protect his family. The emotions rushed through her again, as they had been doing all day, as they would likely continue to do for who knew how long. So much of the day had become a blur for her. Flashes of images, sounds, fighting. She almost longed for the numbness that had allowed her to retreat from the worst of it.

Almost. Shae knew there was no integrity in hiding, no valor in running from problems. As she looked into the cup of tea the sheriff had made her, she saw the reflection of the flickering candles in the room. One small flame would've been too little, but together they lit up the space. Together they made a difference. She might be just one small flame, but she could help Jeb and Aaron, could do something to assist in bringing about the justice she and her children and the memory of her husband deserved.

She looked over at Jeb. The man had been quiet most of the day. Reserved, but still firmly in charge. She was thankful yet again for his taking command of the situation. Within the hour they'd been moved from their home to his, clothing found, the children bathed, the blood washed away. Her cuts and bruises still stung; her body had been abused in so many ways. But the man had said nothing, merely taken her family into his home as if they were his own.

It would be so simple to revel in the solitude, hide in the silence the sheriff was allotting her. But that would accomplish nothing. If she didn't speak now, it would only grow harder as time moved on.

"I'm ready," Shae said, holding the mug of tea to keep her hands from shaking.

Jeb turned slightly in his chair. The man would be intimidating if she hadn't known him so well. He was tall, dark-haired with dark eyes. Someone more than one young lady had called handsome since Shae had known him. But his past, mostly only hinted at in conversations she and Richard had late at night, kept walls up around the lawman. His confidence, sometimes seen as arrogance, was exactly what she needed in the moment. He believed she could be strong and, for whatever reason, she didn't want to let him down.

"I'm not going to make you relive this," Jeb said, setting his cup of coffee on the table between them. "A lot of it we can figure out just fine on our own. What I can't do is see the faces, or hear the words. I know none of this will be pleasant, but you know the things I can't know. Most importantly, who I need to bring in."

"That's the thing, Jeb," she sighed out. "I don't know. I've never seen them before."

"It's all right, Shae. Even that's a good place to start. You said 'them.' How many are we talking?"

"Three," she said without hesitation, her hands subconsciously moving to her wrists.

She saw the man glance down and folded her hands again, trying to shake the image of being held down, violated. Jeb knew the conversation was making her uncomfortable. The woman couldn't sit still. She stood suddenly, took a seat just as often. Wandered from the dining table to the small kitchen behind her, back out past him into the front room.

"I know this was a terrible time," Jeb said. "I can't imagine what you've been through. But if you saw them again, would you be able to recognize them? Was there anything that stood out to you? Scars? Voices? Anything like that?"

The memories flooded back over her. She thought she'd been prepared for it, but the onslaught was overwhelming. Her fear for the baby. Benjamin calling out to his father, trying, again and again, to wake him as the man lay dead on the floor of their home.

"Shae," she heard Jeb whisper. "It's all right. It's over."

He'd been telling her that constantly throughout the day. It was her first clear memory after the chaos had subsided. But it wasn't all right. She didn't know how she could ever feel safe again. Not in that house. Maybe not even in this town. Every time she'd step outside she would wonder who was watching her, if they were coming back. Somehow even worse was that the man before her had seen her at her most vulnerable. She vaguely remembered Aaron bringing her a blanket, but still, that barely covered the embarrassment of being found the way she had been. Naked, shamed, broken.

She forced herself to meet Jeb's eyes across the table.

"None of this will be all right," she said, "until you've found these men and they hang for what they've done. Maybe not even then."

"Good," Jeb surprised her by saying. "Use that anger. They want to make you a victim, but you don't let them. I'll make them pay for this and you are going to be the one to help me do it."

"I don't know what I can do though, Jeb." She felt her voice shake. The emotions came in rapid floods, contradicting one another, fighting for precedent. Fear, anger, shame, guilt. Each moment put another at the forefront of her mind, confusing her thoughts and motivations. "If I saw them, would I recognize them? Yes. At least I believe so. It was just so much all at once. The children, and ... and Richard. He tried to protect us, Jeb, he truly did. But there was just no chance. It was all so sudden. They burst in and ..." her voice faltered at the memory.

"And being a strong woman, you wanted to protect your children," Jeb prompted her gently.

"Yes," she wiped at her eyes. "I had Daisy in her crib ... Benjamin was ..." she looked up at the ceiling, fighting tears. "Benjamin was playing on the floor. They came in and Richard jumped up, you know, trying to get between us and them. I tried to get Benjamin to come to me, but he was scared, Jeb. So scared. Richard argued with the men, tried to get them outside, but then, something happened ... I was" — her voice caught — "I was reaching out for Ben when I heard the shot. Richard fell between us and, I know this is awful, but I thought maybe they would leave then, maybe they had done what they intended and would get away from my children."

Jeb stunned her by reaching across the table and putting his rough, calloused hand on top of hers. She hadn't realized how badly she was shaking until that moment.

"You were both trying to protect the little ones," he said quietly.

"Of course!" she almost shouted the words, then, fearing she would wake the children, lowered her tone. "Of course we were. Richard loved us deeply. And then he was gone. And then ..." She felt her control slipping as she remembered what happened next, the gruffness of the men, the sick laughter as she fought against them while they tore off her clothes, pushed her legs apart ...

"Shae," she could hear Jeb saying. "Shae, you're here now. No one's coming into this house. No one's going to lay a finger on you while I'm still breathing."

His tone cut through her mind. The softness, the gentleness wrapped around an iron resolve. Richard was a protector, to be sure. But he was quick to anger, quick to put it on display. This was different. Jeb wasn't cold, just the opposite. This approach, though — his gentleness was something she hadn't experienced before.

Shae looked at the man. "I believe you," she said, her voice still wavering slightly.

"How about we wrap this up for now?" Jeb suggested.

"But, I ..."

What? What did she really want to say? The truth was, Jeb had gotten to the heart of what she didn't even know she was feeling. She just wanted the day to be over.

"Like I was saying before," the sheriff began, "I've got more than enough room for you here. This house is probably too big for one fella on his own, anyway. You go on upstairs and get some rest with the young 'uns. I'll take care of everything else."

"I thank you for your hospitality, sincerely," Shae said. "In the morning, I'll look for somewhere we can stay until ..."

Until when? She didn't know if she could ever set foot in that house again.

Jeb stood and gathered their mugs from the table. "Let's not worry about that for the time being. If it eases your conscience, you just tell yourself I want you here so I know you're safe. If you feel better calling it a favor, well, you can do that as well. Whatever you wanna call it, you just plan on staying here until we come up with a plan we all like."

"All right." She moved toward the stairs gingerly. Her body begged her for rest; every muscle ached. But she wanted to say something more than a "thank you.' The words seemed too simple, too light for what had happened that day.

She watched him move calmly around the house, willing some of his confidence to encourage the same in her.

He looked over his shoulder at her. "Get some rest, Shae. I'll be right here if you need anything."

Shae nodded and walked up the stairs toward the room where her children slept. Rest might be a task easier said than done, she thought. But somehow, she felt the sheriff's presence just might make it possible.

Chapter Two

A few days later, Jeb was out at the stable, brushing down his Appaloosa after another long day of riding the dusty territory. The open spaces of northern Texas had always been where he'd gone to think. In some places, the land stretched out so far all he could see was the flat, unbroken horizon. In others, rolling hills and red rock formations stood up proudly.

Benjamin was perched on a hay bale a few feet away, asking the barrage of questions that all young children seem to have, interjecting "why?" after each one.

Jeb smiled. He remembered these exchanges, the half smiling, half exhausted looks his wife would give him, her eyebrows up as if to say, "Can't you calm this child?" He had always laughed then, and he laughed now at the memory. Children were insatiable, but he supposed a part of him had never lost that need to know either. Back then it had been, how could he improve the ranch? How could he be a better provider? How could he look out for his family?

But things had changed. One afternoon could change so much. It had suddenly become, how could someone do this? How could they take his family? How could he hunt them down? And as Benjamin kept asking, so had Jeb himself asked, why? Why him? Why his wife and children? Why his life?

Yes, he thought, an afternoon could change so much.

Benjamin seemed to be bouncing back okay so far. Younger children usually did. Daisy, the blessed girl, would have no recollection of events at all. But still, she'd grow with that absence in her life, that wonder about what her father had been like, and what had happened when she was still too small to understand anything beyond hunger and fatigue.

"Why?" Benjamin asked.

Jeb looked over at the boy, running back through the questions he'd been asked before his mind had begun to wander. Then he remembered:

Ah, yes, the horse.

"Well," Jeb said, "that's a pretty good question, but I'll tell ya, I'm not the one to ask. For that one, you're gonna have to talk to our friend Aaron. He knows all there is to know about the animals around here."

"Why?"

"You see," Jeb said as he set the brush down and hunkered down in front of the boy, "Aaron knows all the tribes around these parts. It's like he's one of them."

"Why?"

"Because he's a good man. And no matter where you go, you grow up to be a good man, and you'll find friends there. Aaron is good to the people here and they respect it. So much, in fact, sometimes they tell him their stories and secrets."

"And they know why he has spots?" Ben pointed at the horse.

"If anybody knows, they know. And if they know, I bet ya Aaron knows."

Benjamin hopped up off the hay bale, presumably to go find Aaron and the answer to his questions. "Where is he?"

Jeb stood up, cracking his back. "Oh, I reckon he's probably at his house, sitting down to a dinner about now."

"Why?"

"Because it's supper time." Jeb reached over and put his hat on the small boy's head. "Aren't you hungry?"

Ben shrugged and removed the hat, looking at it from every angle. Just then, the clang of the dinner bell could be heard from the front porch. Jeb hadn't heard it ring in years.

Benjamin looked up at him, surprised at the sound.

"Best sound in the world right there," Jeb said, putting his hand on the boy's shoulder to encourage him to walk to the house. "Chow time."

"Why?"

***

After dinner, before Jeb could even begin to start cleaning up, Shae had already gathered the dishes and shooed Benjamin outside to wash up at the pump. The boy, of course, had needed to know the reasons behind this, but Shae, impressing Jeb very much, had deftly turned the chore into a challenge, encouraging the boy's eagerness to show just how clean and how quick he could be.

"You've surely got that one pegged," Jeb said, watching Benjamin out the window.

"I was the only girl in a family of boys." Shae smiled. "I had to figure things out pretty quick just to survive."

Jeb watched her tidying up. Survive. It was a good word for her. And a skill she'd clearly learned well. Not that the past days had been easy — far from it. But he'd kept an eye on her, both as a lawman and as a friend, and the woman had shown remarkable strength in her recovery from tragedy. He hadn't pushed anything on her since that first night, assuming she knew he was there when or if she wanted to talk.

Maybe it wasn't the way most sheriffs would handle the situation, but, as he often thought, he hadn't set out to be a sheriff to begin with. If his ways were a little unorthodox, well then, so be it.

"I wanted to say I appreciate all the helping out you been doing around here," Jeb said, stretching out his legs at the table. "You're gonna spoil me, though."

Shae glanced over at him and smiled briefly. "I'm not one to just sit on my hands," she said. "And besides, you're doing much more for us than I could possibly do for you. A single man taking on a widow and her two children ..."

She'd used the word only a time or two. Jeb had avoided it entirely. Not using the term wouldn't change the situation, of course, but he didn't feel any strong need to label her as such. Perhaps she was trying to force herself to stay in the reality of it all. She couldn't stay in his home forever, after all. She had a family to raise. Needed to get out and find a new man someday. Hunkering down in his home was certainly where he preferred her at this time. With no clear idea of exactly who it was that had burst in and ruined this woman's life, Jeb wasn't too keen on letting her very far out of his sight, if he could help it. Every new face he saw in town, he immediately had to wonder, was it this man? That one? Who would've done such a thing?

No, for the time being, Shae was right where she needed to be. After Jeb tracked down who did this, brought them to justice, or put a bullet in them — either was fine with him — then he and Shae could start thinking about finding a new place for her and the children.

Then again, he thought, it had been nice having a woman around the house again. He'd enjoyed looking down to realize little Ben had snuck up on him. Even holding the baby while

Shae had been busy. He'd missed being a part of a family. Maybe, after a time …

No, he shook the thought away. This was his dead deputy's wife. These were Richard's children. Jeb would do right by them, but he needed to make sure he did so in an honorable way.

"I'm gonna be heading out with Aaron most of the day again tomorrow," Jeb said, trying to get his mind back on work. "I can arrange to have some folks drop by throughout the day, if you'd like."

Shae paused in her work, wiping her forehead with the back of her hand. "Oh, good. So now not only am I inconveniencing you, I'm inconveniencing everyone within riding distance of here."

"Don't think of it that way," Jeb said. "You aren't any trouble to me or anybody else. Fact is, I ain't had a house so clean in years. And I don't know if I've ever eaten like this."

"I need to do something," the woman said. Jeb wasn't sure if this was her way of earning her rent and board or if she meant it with regard to her own ability to get up each day. Either way, she was right. A woman like her didn't take to sitting around. Seeing her up and moving was more than he would've hoped for so soon, given the situation.

"All right," Jeb said. "Well, I don't reckon me and Aaron will be out too late. Not if this is the kinda dinner I got waiting on me when I get back."

Jeb saw her smile and blush slightly.

"I'd leave you instructions for the place in case you need anything while I'm out, but I'd say you know it just about as well as I do at this point. You need anything else, got neighbors within a stone's throw both ways."

He knew she knew this. He'd said it to her over and over since she'd been staying there. But the more he could ingrain those thoughts in her, the more he could remind her that she wasn't alone, the better off he hoped things would be.

Still, though, it wouldn't hurt to stop by a few places and arrange for some visits while he was away. Richard had been a popular man in town, friendly with just about everybody. No sense in leaving the woman on her own in these times.

"Oh!" He glanced up at the woman's outburst, then followed her gaze out the window. "That boy!"

Jeb stood up. "I'll handle this one."

"Thank you," Shae said.

"Won't be the first boy I pulled out of a mud hole." Jed grinned and headed to the door.

Chapter Three

The next morning, Jeb met Aaron at the Tulley cabin just after the sun had risen. In such a short time, the place had already taken on a feeling of foreboding, a lingering essence of the terrible deeds that had taken place there. Jeb had asked Aaron to ride by sporadically, and had done so as well himself, not so much expecting to apprehend anyone but curious to see who would come looking. The place had remained desolate and, Jeb thought, likely would be if no one moved in soon. But a house that had borne witness to some things was often left to rot in its own time.

Aaron was hitching his horse to the porch rail and Jeb, dismounting, did the same.

"Any better ideas of what we oughtta be looking for?" Aaron asked.

Jeb shook his head slowly. "Nah, I'm trying to let her talk in her own time. And she has been, slowly. To be frank, I was hoping these fellows would've slipped up, been seen by somebody a little less scared outta their wits. But from what I've heard around town, it was like ghosts. You?"

"Same. I keep thinking there's got to be something we aren't seeing. But he was a lawman. People don't come after us, not like this anyway. But that also means it probably wasn't about money or land. Richard had a good head on his shoulders, but you can't spin gold outta wheat. I figure he was sitting on the same amount of cash socked away as me, or thereabouts, and I'm not saying I'm scraping the bottom of the barrel, but it ain't enough for what those men did here."

"Yeah," Jeb said. "I tend to agree. Money and land. Those are the two things men want out here." He looked around the plot of the homestead. "And neither one of 'em is in too much abundance where we're standing."

Aaron sighed. "I just keep thinking it's gotta be something, though. Maybe I just don't wanna think that men could come in and do this at random, but ..."

"No," Jeb replied. "They talked to Richard about something. Shae remembers at least that much. She didn't catch what they was talking about, of course, but it wasn't just a random bit of violence. They wanted Richard specifically."

"But why?"

"That is the question," Jeb mused. "Tell you what, you got the training for it; why don't you do a little walkabout, see if you can't find something amiss out here. I'll go over the indoors again."

Aaron scratched at his neck. The young man had spent the better part of his youth in the company of the Comanche tribe indigenous to the area. It had caused more than a bit of head-scratching, not only by the whites at Aaron's intense interest in the people, but in their seeming unquestioning acceptance of him. Perhaps they saw a bit of a kindred spirit in the youth. Jeb had known Aaron all his life, had seen the hard upbringing, had been one of the few who knew where Aaron was disappearing to for hours, then days, and as they grew weeks and months at a time.

But there was a peace between the youth and the natives. He'd learned their language, studied their customs and traditions. And Jeb was thankful to know Aaron had become one of the best trackers in the area, not just among the settlers, but among any of the people who passed through it. If there was anything to be found outside, Aaron would do it.

Jeb watched as the other man tilted his cowboy hat back, walked to the edge of the porch and hunkered down, looking among the sparse grass for signs that were invisible to others. Meanwhile, Jeb turned to the inside of the house.

The interior sat in the same disarray it had since Jeb had first arrived, which had both good and bad aspects to it. On the one hand, any clue he may have overlooked in his previous investigations should likely still be there awaiting his eye. On the other, nothing new was nothing new. No one was coming by searching for something. No new boot tracks or evidence that could tie a person to this place had turned up. Not for the first time, Jeb considered spending a night in the place, sending Aaron back on with his horse later and waiting in the seemingly empty home to see if anyone came calling.

But, he knew he couldn't leave Shae alone like that. Not that the woman wasn't strong, it was more simply the matter that Jeb felt better when he was there to keep an eye on her, ready if she needed him.

Jeb walked slowly around the room, examining the broken furniture, the dead ashes in the fireplace, the corner where Shae had been. Not a splinter had moved. He tested his weight on the floorboards, hoping for a telltale squeak that might indicate a loose board concealing a potential hiding place, but the home was sturdy as ever. What could Richard have had that anyone would want? To the best of Shae's knowledge, the men had left empty-handed. And to the best of Jeb's recollection, nothing seemed to be missing, even with the chaos inside.

He could hear Aaron working his way around the outside of the house. If it had been anyone else, Jeb would've been concerned the man was moving too quickly for a proper search. But having worked beside Aaron as long as he had, the man's efficiency was one thing he truly appreciated.

About that time, Aaron called out to him. "We got 'em, Jeb."

His voice wasn't loud or even overly emotional, more a simple, grim fact. Both men had been waiting for the clue that would point them in any direction at all, and now, finally, Aaron had found something. Jeb hurried outside and around to the back of the house where Aaron stood, hands on his hips, looking off into the distance and then back down to his feet again. He glanced over as Jeb walked up beside him.

"Right here," Aaron said. "I'm not terribly surprised I didn't see it before, though that don't make me feel much better about it. The light on this side is tricky, you see?" He knelt down and at what, to Jeb, looked like just another patch of dirt in a patchy, thirsty plot of Texas land. Seeing Jeb's uncertainty, Aaron traced a shape in the air above the dirt. "Right here. They came around same way you did. Probably after everything, I imagine. No need to act suspicious till they'd committed the crimes, I suppose. Exit the way you're least likely to be seen."

Jeb nodded. The men had come through the front door, Shae had confirmed that, but then left by cutting across the empty grasslands behind. That would explain why no one had noticed them; on this side of town, there was nothing worth seeing between Richard's back door and Oklahoma.

"Can you tell how many?" Jeb asked. Shae had told him three, but for all he knew, the men had split ways right here, making his job three times harder. But then again, all he needed was one man breathing enough still to talk.

"All of 'em, looks like," Aaron said, straightening back up. "I reckon Shae was right when she said three. I thought maybe there'd been a lookout, something, but from what the ground says, they came around here, stopped for a moment to get their bearings most likely, and took off that way." He pointed off into the distance where a small wood could be seen at the horizon. "You wanna gather up some men or head out?"

"No time like the present," Jeb said, walking around the corner of the house toward his mount. Truth be told, there was no time to lose.

***

Just inside the edge of the woods, the two men found an old animal track that led them to a worn, but still used, footpath. Aaron had gestured for them to dismount, and the pair crept through the underbrush slowly along the edge of the path. Jeb followed behind, keeping an eye ahead, behind, and to their sides, as Aaron moved with silent quickness, his eyes keeping them in line with the marks and signs of the recent travelers they sought.

After a few hundred yards, Aaron halted, held up a hand, and gestured for Jeb to hunker down beside him. Just ahead of them, in a small clearing, sat a dilapidated, but currently occupied, shack. Aaron pointed to one side, holding up three fingers to indicate the three horses hitched to a rail there. Voices could be heard drifting through the air and the faintest wisp of smoke twisted from the chimney.

Jeb leaned down to whisper to the man. "They been here all this time, odds are they ain't been too far from the bottle. We can head back and get some extra hands if you want, but I'm betting me and you can get the jump on 'em and have this over with before they know what hit 'em."

Aaron smiled. "The odds look good to me, boss. You go left, I go right?"

Jeb looked up at the shack. There were windows on either side of the door, but they were dirty with disuse. The two lawmen could likely slip by unnoticed and take up positions on either side of the door without trouble. "Sounds good," Jeb said.

Aaron slipped out from cover, running low. After a few paces, Jeb followed him, a hand on the butt of his revolver. As they covered the short distance, the voices grew louder, clearer, and to Jeb's ears, more drunken. Given the early hour, it was unlikely the men were up already. More likely, he and Aaron were sneaking up on the end of the previous night's activities.

The two silently stole to the front door, standing with their backs against the wood, guns drawn and ready. At a signal, Jeb beat on the old door. "Sheriff!"

The voices died down, as if perhaps through silence they could suddenly be hidden, forgotten.

"Y'all can come on out, or we can come in," Jeb said. "Don't make no difference to us."

There was a somewhat clumsy shuffle from inside, the sound of men too inebriated to be sneaky attempting to spread out and prepare themselves for a fight.

"That's about what I figured," Jeb sighed.

Aaron crept over to the window on his side and slowly poked his head up, attempting to see through the dirty glass. Almost immediately a shot rang out, shattering the glass as Aaron ducked back down. "Looks like they made their choice, boss," the deputy said, brushing some glass shards from his jeans with the barrel of his gun.

"Reckon so," Jeb said. Then, raising his voice, he yelled to the men inside. "You've fired on an officer of the law! So, we'll be coming in now!"

He locked eyes with Aaron and at the same moment, the deputy fired back through the window as Jeb kicked in the front door. The gunfire was brief, intense, and over almost as quickly as it had begun. Smoke left a haze in the room, but the unmistakable sounds of victory came to Jeb's ear. A cry of pain, a curse, the thunk of two revolvers hitting the floor at his feet.

A moan came from somewhere off to his left, and as the air cleared, Jeb stood boldly at the center of the room. To his left one man lay, clearly dead, Aaron's bullet either by luck or skill having found the man's heart. To his right another was doubled over, clutching at a wound in his shoulder. The third stood directly ahead of the sheriff, arms held high and eyes wide. A few empty bottles rolled noisily across the wooden floor.

"We need to talk to you boys about Richard Tulley," Jeb said as he heard Aaron come through the door behind him. "You're coming back with us one way or another, so what say we just make this easy on everybody?"

The man in front of him nodded; the one to his side cursed, but both were quickly in cuffs and being led out to their horses where Aaron helped them into the saddles and took control of their reins.

Chapter Four

Back in the sheriff's station, Jeb had the wounded man tended to by the local doctor. "Bullet went right through. No matter what he tells ya, all he's got to worry about is the pain," the doctor had said, earning a sneer from the criminal. The two were then tossed in separate cells across from one another. Given the wound of the one and the rather compliant attitude of the other, Jeb wasn't overly concerned about schemes or escapes, but the solitude, even in proximity, gave him a slight edge over the men psychologically.

He stood in the hall between the cells, looking back and forth. He and Aaron had discussed the questioning already, but the more he was able to assert his authority, the more likely one of them would be to break. Thankfully, the two had already made it very clear which that would be, and Jeb only lingered for a moment before pulling the unharmed man out to the front of the office, sitting him in a chair across the desk with Aaron at his back, and settling into his own.

Jeb looked quietly over at the man. Often, he'd found, simply waiting was all it took to break a man's resolve. This fellow proved to be no different. After only a few minutes under Jeb's gaze, the man became restless, shifting in his chair, eyes darting around the room.

"Whatever miracle you're hoping for," Jeb said, "it ain't coming. Your best chance now is to sit right there and spill your guts. More you tell me now, the less I'm gonna have to find out on my own. More I know you're trying to help me out, well, the more I can tell the judge you was trying to do the right thing." Jeb watched as the man clenched his jaw, the last futile efforts at resistance fighting inside him. "Maybe you think that won't make much difference," Jeb said. "And maybe you're right. If it was up to me, I'd just as soon see ya hang right now. But I ain't the judge nor the executioner. You can trust me though, friend, that noose don't care how tough you acted right here."

As if on cue, Aaron walked up to the edge of the desk, sitting down on its corner. "Other guy might have something to say," he said nonchalantly. "Sides, I's hoping to get home for dinner tonight. This one don't wanna talk, we can get it out of his partner."

The criminal looked between the two men, his resolve finally giving way. "All right," he said, looking down at his hands. "All right, but look" — he glanced back up at Jeb — "I want you to know I didn't have nothing to do with what happened to that woman. Not with the killin' either. I's told we go in, scare 'im some, let the boss deal with the rest."

Aaron held out his hands and moved back to his place behind the outlaw.

"Seems like we might be able to get somewhere now," Jeb leaned forward. "That woman and that man. You know who they are? Who they were?"

The man shrugged. "Boss just sends us out. I don't ask no questions. He don't like that."

"I see," Jeb said, settling back in his chair. "So the boss just tells you where to go, what to do, and you jump? That about right?"

Chagrined at the simplistic, if accurate description, the man nodded, hanging his head.

"Risky way to live a life," Jeb said. "For all you knew that warn't no family in there. Coulda been anybody. Coulda been a group of fellers waiting on you."

The man seemed to think about this for a moment, as if it were the first time he'd questioned the blind loyalty he'd been acting under. "Yeah," he said. "Yeah, I reckon you's right."

"Some might call that brave," Jeb said. "In a certain situation, I might even call that brave." The man looked up, for the briefest moment something almost like hope flashing in his eyes. Then Jeb continued. "But I call it foolish. Worse than foolish, willingly stupid. Because what you done, friend, not what you was supposed to do and not what you was thinking you'd do, but what you done, is you shot one of my deputies."

Jeb waited for a moment, allowing the full heft of the words to sink in. He watched the man's eyes widen, the depth of the crime growing.

"I don't know if it's better or worse for you, or her," Jeb said, "that the man's wife is still alive. But I'll tell you one thing, nothing'd make her happier than to dance on your grave. And to tell you another thing, I don't blame her a bit. If it was up to me, I'da shot all three of you out there and left ya to coyotes or to the rot. Whichever don't matter much to me."

Aaron caught Jeb's eye over the man's shoulder. Judging by the deputy's expression, Jeb knew he'd worn the man down enough, made his point fully. To push too much farther could be risky; the man might decide it didn't matter if he talked or not, or he might get so flustered he'd admit to anything just in the hopes of avoiding the rope.

Jeb turned his head one way, then the other, cracking the vertebrae in his neck. "But that ain't neither here nor there at the moment. We've got bigger fish to fry, as they say. And the first fish I'd like to hear about is this boss of yours. You keep saying he's runnin' things, but you ain't happened to mention a name yet. He got one?"

"Yeah," the man muttered, then looked up at the sheriff. "Yes, sir. He do. Goes by Vanderheist."

Jeb glanced up at Aaron, who nodded. The name was new to Jeb, but Aaron seemed to have some kind of information. Things were finally starting to look up. Not only did they have two of the culprits, Aaron would be able to verify any of the stories this man decided to try and sell them.

"Vanderheist, eh?" Jeb said. "That's a name we been hearing 'round here. You wanna elaborate for us? Maybe you got some details we don't."

"Well," the man said, clearly wanting to help now, "it's like I said. He usually just tells us what to do, and ..."

"Who's us?" Jeb asked. "Just you three?"

"Well there's a ..." The man fidgeted in his seat. "See, there's fellers all over work for Mr. Vanderheist. I don't know 'em all. Not by a long shot."

"So, how do you know there are any? Perhaps it's just you," Jeb said.

"People, they, well, they talk, sir," the man said. "And what Mr. Vanderheist gets into, assuming it's as true as they say, well, he'd need a lotta men for it. He ain't just interested in Amarillo, see? He's all over."

"I do see," Jeb said. "This Mr. Vanderheist, where might I be able to find him?"

The man's eyes grew fearful again. "I don't know that, sheriff. I really don't. I ain't never seen him in the same place twice."

"But surely you were planning on seeing him again?"

"We was told to get to that shack and hunker down," the man said. "That's all I knowed about it. Swear on the good book."

Jeb smirked a little at the expression.

"Honest," the man hurried on. "Said we was to go talk to that feller, the deputy of yours you say, and then Vanderheist, he told us about that shack and said lay low till we heard from him."

"So, he was coming out himself?"

The man shook his head. "No, maybe. I don't know, see? That's part of it. Vanderheist, he don't like you knowing too much of anything. He tells you do something, you do. Like I said. Alls I knowed was we was to go to that shack and sit tight. Maybe Vanderheist'd come. Maybe somebody else. Maybe nobody and he figured we'd get stir crazy enough to wander off after a week or so. But that's all I knowed we was supposed to do."

Jeb glanced back at Aaron, who simply nodded.

"All right," Jeb said. "That'll do for now. I'll give ya bit of advice, seeing as how you claim you didn't know any better and was just doin' what you was told."

The man looked up at him.

"When you get back there to that cell, you might not wanna tell your buddy you was up here taking orders and doing as you were told. He may not like that too much."

"Yes, sir," the man said as Aaron helped him up by the elbow and led him back to the cells.

Jeb watched from his desk, waiting for Aaron to return so they could review the information. He didn't want to buy the man's story. But at the same time, who in their right mind would go into a deputy's home and do what they did? Whoever this Vanderheist was, he knew enough to choose his men half-wisely, dumb enough to be brave. What concerned Jeb was that the boss seemed brave enough to be dumb. Those men were sometimes the most dangerous.

Aaron rounded the corner and sat down in the chair previously occupied by the culprit.

"What do you think?" Jeb asked.

Aaron shrugged. "Seems to hold up with what I been hearing. Nothing real solid on the man, otherwise I'da said something sooner about it. But he's one of those names you hear floating around."

"I ain't heard it."

"You ain't out with the folks I know."

Jeb nodded. "I see. What's the word with our native friends?"

"Not much," Aaron said. "They ain't real big on sharing their concerns most the time anyway, but from what I heard, some white man, some call him just 'The German,' some call him by his name, or some form of it … I've heard Vanderhoff, Vinderberg, but all of 'em close enough for us, I'd bet, but they treat him almost like a ghost."

"Ghost he ain't." Jeb smirked.

"No, that he ain't," Aaron agreed. "But you talk to ten different folks, you get ten different versions. One thing for sure, though, Jeb, he ain't just kicking up dust in our neck, even up in the north. He's getting all the way over into New Mexico Territory. Sounds like whatever he's working on, it ain't no local problem. It's big."

Jeb folded his hands and leaned back in his chair. "Big is right," he said quietly. "What in the Sam Hill did Richard get himself into?"

"Wish I knew, boss," Aaron said.

"Tell ya what," Jeb said, leaning forward on the desk. "Now that we've got a name, I want you to get out and start asking around. If they think he's a ghost, ask about the ghost. If they don't know the name, you find out if they know something anyway. We figure out what this man's after, we're one step closer to solving this thing."

"You coming with?" Aaron asked. On occasion Jeb had ridden along, attempting to build a formal, if not friendly, relationship with the tribespeople.

"Not this time," Jeb said.

Aaron looked at him. "You're going back out to the house, ain't ya?"

"There's something there," Jeb said. "I don't know what, but why go after a man in his home like that? Richard was out all over this area during the day. Why not drag him down out there?"

"Send a message?" Aaron suggested.

"Maybe," Jeb said. "But I think there's more to it than that."

"Well," Aaron stood, adjusting his hat. "Whatever you find out, you be sure and let me know. You ain't the only one wanting to get to the bottom of this."

"Likewise," Jeb said.

Aaron nodded and headed out the door to his horse. He could return that evening or not until the next day. Jeb knew the indigenous people kept their own schedules, their own traditions. But in the meantime, he needed to get back out to the Tulley place before heading back to Shae.

Chapter Five

Edward Vanderheist stood at the end of the bar in the Horsehoe Saloon. His back was straight, his suit crisp, but his patience wearing thin. The man across from him, Lewis, has been taking an attitude Vanderheist never appreciated, which was any attitude outside of exact, prompt compliance. What people didn't seem to understand, or to not fully grasp, was that money didn't simply fall out of Vanderheist's pockets. He was a made man who'd seen an opportunity in this new country and he had taken advantage of it. He'd worked to get where he was and those who took it lightly often found the consequences rather on the dire end of the spectrum.

Perhaps, he thought for the thousandth time, guns and alcohol truly didn't mix. But then again, with the ever-expanding westward movement of the American people, outside of food and shelter, guns and alcohol seemed to present the greatest need. And Edward Vanderheist happened to be the man who could supply. If things went according to plan. If he didn't have to deal with attitudes like Lewis was portraying. If he could find men more reliable than that less than useless deputy he'd had to deal with.

"Lewis," Vanderheist interrupted. He hadn't necessarily been listening, but whatever the man was going to say, or had been saying, Edward was sure he'd heard it a dozen times from a hundred different associates. Things were moving slowly, or things were too risky. Things were too expensive. Always things that, unsurprisingly, were out of the associate's hands, and if he could simply spare some more time, etc., etc., etc.

"Lewis," Vanderheist repeated, holding up a hand. "I didn't come in here today to discuss the minutiae. That is your end of things, as I believe I made clear. You are the man in the street; I am the man giving the orders. If you don't feel up to the task of following these orders, I can assure you I will have no problem moving my business elsewhere. What that means for you, frankly, I do not care. I do not care about your problems. I do not care about your excuses. I am not your friend. We are involved with one another for one reason only, to make money. The moment that ceases to occur, we are no longer in need of one another." He paused. "Or, at least, I am no longer in need of you."

The bartender paused for a moment, a look of confusion on his face. Whether that was surprise at the blatant description of his expendability or, more likely, Vanderheist thought, an onslaught of words containing more than one syllable, was really irrelevant. All Vanderheist needed the man to know was that he was not in charge. This was not Lewis's deal and never had been.

Just as Vanderheist was about to commence with his closing remarks, a commotion in the saloon behind him drew his attention. A dusty, dirty man raced across the room. While the unkempt appearance was not in the least unusual for the area — though Vanderheist couldn't stand the filth — the man's direction, a bee-line toward the German himself, did seem out of character. Edward Vanderheist was not a man who made threats, simply due to the fact he had never needed to. And his actions spoke loudly enough to encourage nearly all men to give him a wide berth.

As the fellow approached though, Edward felt his jaw clench. This could not be anything but more bad news on an already highly irritating day.

"Boss," the man said, leaning on the bar and attempting to catch his breath.

Vanderheist looked at him for a moment, allowing his disgust at the interruption to make itself known.

"I wouldn'ta come, sir," the man panted, "but it's bad."

Vanderheist looked the man up and down. Trevor, yes, that was his name. And he should've been nowhere near the Horseshoe Saloon. Edward looked back to Lewis.

"As you can see, you are not the only problem I have to deal with in a day," he said to the bartender. "But you are certainly one I can eliminate. Bear that in mind and consider this a miraculous reprieve. Get your affairs in order. I'll return in twenty-four hours and I expect progress. If all you have is more excuses by this time tomorrow, I would suggest not lingering for my arrival, though I also wouldn't get your hopes too high that you can't be found. My reach is wide, Lewis, and those who are loyal to me know no bounds."

He turned to Trevor. "Now then, if you're done making a spectacle of yourself, let's sit for a moment."

As they turned toward a table, Vanderheist was almost but not quite certain he heard the bartender mutter something under his breath. Edward paused for a moment, filing the remark away for later use, and then led his man to an empty chair.

Trevor slumped down into his seat; Vanderheist sat, crossed one leg over the other, and rested a chin in his hand. "I have to presume this must be of utmost importance," he said.

The man nodded. "My apologies, boss, sincerest. I know you hate being bothered, but the thing is ... well ..."

"Perhaps you can begin with explaining why you aren't at the cabin. I'm quite sure I was abundantly clear on your instructions."

"That's the thing," Trevor said. "We was there, like you said. Holed up, everything was going smoothly. Nobody came near that place the first day or so."

"I get the distinct feeling this is going to end with some kind of drunkenness," Vanderheist said. "If so, please do skip the introductory remarks."

"Well, yeah," the man said. "There was some drinking; I'll admit to that."

Edward smiled. *Admit it,* he thought, *as if I wouldn't find out anyway.*

"But you see," Trevor continued, "I was out hunting early this morning. You know how you gotta be out before the sun and all. Well, I was out, see, and finally 'bout to give up. Ain't nothing out that way to begin with. But I's coming back and I hear something coming through the brush. I figured, hell, maybe it's a coyote or some such. Ain't good eating but I ain't shot nothing neither."

Vanderheist felt his lip curl up, at the man's suggestion of eating coyote as much as at his grammar. Edward had learned the language just fine; it baffled him how many of the countrymen couldn't be bothered to do the same.

"So, I hunkered down," Trevor was saying. "But it warn't no coyote or nothing. It was them other two lawmen. The sheriff and his Indian boy."

Edward leaned forward, ignoring the obvious error in description. "They found you?"

"I told you that feller'd track a sneeze in a dust storm."

"And?"

"And they snuck up to the shack real quiet-like. Our boys tried to fight 'em off, but sheriff got the drop on 'em. Ole Nick caught a bullet in the heart. Clark and Smitty got hauled off."

"I see," Vanderheist mused. "And that, of course, leaves you. Watching from the bushes, was it?"

"It was so fast, boss. Time I realized what was going down they done had it finished. If I'da had the shot, I'da taken it."

"Would you have, though?" Vanderheist leaned back in his chair. "Because, to be frank, it seems a more level-headed decision to stay out of the jail, stay away from two more dead lawmen, and bring the problem to someone who knows how to handle these types of things."

"Well," Trevor paused for a moment. "Yeah! Yeah, that's what I was thinking while I was there."

Vanderheist sighed. Had he really just attempted to intimidate Lewis with tales of his crack team? But, often one had to take what one could get. "So, in short, of your gang, one is dead, two are in lock-up, and you are here. Wonderful."

"I just wanted to know what to do, boss."

The German held his chin in his hand for a moment, thinking. "To be honest, Trevor, I believe we only have one choice. Perhaps you're coming here will be a bit redundant, given that you could've simply solved this problem on your own. But I do commend your attempt to follow some kind of chain of command."

"Thank ya kindly."

The pair sat in silence for a moment till Trevor finally spoke up. "So, what's the plan?"

"Simple," Vanderheist said. "We need to remove these other two lawmen from the equation. It simply won't be good for business otherwise."

Trevor smiled, his teeth stained dark from chewing tobacco. "I'm with ya there, boss."

***

Meanwhile, on the front porch of Jeb's home, Shae sat with a woman from down the street. Having lived on opposite sides of Amarillo, Shae had never made the acquaintance of most of the folks around these parts. Unfortunately, this put her at somewhat of a disadvantage even before everything around her had been taken away. Being the wife of a deputy was not exactly akin to being famous, but in a town like Amarillo, where the law was upheld and the lawmen respected, Shae often found herself being greeted by faces unfamiliar to her, though they were somehow familiar to her husband.

After the attack at their home, word had spread quickly. Jeb had done a commendable job of keeping a balance in his home. She knew he'd asked neighbors to check in; she knew he worried over her more than he let on. But, she had to admit, there was a part of her that thought he had done exactly the right thing. This new woman, Grace Allen, had shown up quite out of the blue, but with an armload of corn and a head full of gossip. The women had sat, shucking corn, trading tales, and laughing — *Laughing!* Shae thought — for the better part of two hours.

Grace, though she might come off as a bit flighty to some, knew exactly what she was doing as much as Jeb did, and Shae inwardly blessed them both for their tact and intuition. Shae knew she needed to talk, knew she would talk eventually. But being the wounded sheep did not sit with her well, either.

With Daisy asleep inside her crib, and Benjamin fighting a losing battle against an afternoon nap in the rocking chair to her side, Shae had finally found a moment's peace after the horror she'd gone through so recently. Yes, she'd slept, but poorly, waking in a cold sweat, reaching out to protect her children, a scream caught on her lips. She'd eaten; she knew she had to keep her strength. No matter what she was dealing with, her two children couldn't survive without her and she had no intentions of imposing on Jeb any longer than she had to. But sleeping, eating, going through the motions of normalcy, even with Jeb himself, were no comparison to the feeling of running her hands down the corn cobs, slipping the silks away as she'd done so many times before. Plucking at the tiny worms hidden away. Watching the pile of shucks grow on one side as the bucket of cleaned ears filled between them. The motions, the regularity, allowed her to shut off that part of her brain that hadn't stopped running since that night everything had changed.

"You know I'm just down the street," Grace said, not looking away from the corncob in her hand. "If you ever want some woman time. And I'm not gonna go telling tales out of school."

Shae laughed. "Then what have we been doing all this time?"

Grace looked over, grinning. "Well, I'm just making sure you're an informed woman."

"I'm more than that," Shae laughed, then seeing a figure coming down the road, waved.

"He's a good man," Grace said, looking out as Jeb approached.

"Yes," Shae said. "Yes, he is."

Chapter Six

The next day, Jeb stood in the middle of the desecrated home. Still nothing had changed in his surroundings, but still he felt sure there was something he wasn't seeing. He knew Aaron would be out with the Comanche all day, perhaps longer, one could never be sure how long these trips would last. But it gave Jeb the uninterrupted and undistracted hours he might need to work his way through the mess and, if nothing else, appease his nagging conscience that kept insisting there was something here still waiting to be found.

Having no better option, he resolved to start at the door and work his way counterclockwise around the building, overturning everything yet again, or perhaps righting it as best he could for the inevitable time he'd need to come back with Shae and see what was left of her belongings that they could salvage. It was an emotional task, not only because of the violence that had occurred, but because of the happy memories he'd shared with the family here as well. Richard and Jeb hadn't been the closest of friends, no one was as close to Jeb as Aaron had been, especially over the last few years, but Richard had been a reliable man, often funny, perhaps a bit quick to anger, but everyone had his faults.

As Jeb moved through the large front room, he was still baffled as to what the men could've been after. On the initial call to the home, Jeb had made his way around in a similar, if more cursory fashion. The two rooms upstairs, a bedroom for Shae and Richard, and one for the children had remained completely undisturbed, so not for the first time, Jeb wondered if what he was looking for had already been removed from the house. But, still, there was that need to know driving him on. Perhaps it was just the audacity of the attack, but nothing about the situation felt right. At least, as right as a rape and murder could feel. He didn't think he was getting too old for the job, but the closeness of this case brought on more feelings than any case had in a long time.

Having made his way past the place Richard died, stepping gingerly over the blood-stained spot on the floorboards, Jeb had continued to set the furniture back in place, creating a small pile in the middle of the room containing the broken items. Some might be repairable, but most were destroyed beyond use. He came to the corner where Shae had been huddled with her children. Now, empty, it seemed nearly untouched amid the chaos of the cabin. Ironic, when one considered perhaps the greatest evil had been done in this very spot.

Jeb worked forward, testing floorboards again, running his fingers along the mortar in the fireplace stones, trying to find anything that could've served as a hiding place. *Maybe there isn't anything*, his mind taunted him. *Maybe the message was all they needed to deliver.*

But if that was the case, why kill the man? Shae didn't seem to know any more about the men's motive than Jeb did, so no actionable insight was clear. Maybe simply information was what they were after, something Richard had known and given up, thereby making himself no longer useful to the gang. It was starting to feel like the only logical answer, but it only raised more questions. What could Richard have known that was worth his life and his wife's honor?

Jeb thought back through the cases they'd worked in the past, the men they'd brought in. Amarillo wasn't unlike most western towns. It had its regular number of bar brawls and drunken show-downs, the latter usually ending in more of a frightening spectacle of stray bullets than a cold-blooded duel to the death outsiders seemed to imagine them being. About half the time Jeb had been involved, the men had either stared one another down, neither wanting to be the first to draw and incur the weight of the law, or had simply talked themselves out of it. The town had grown a reputation as peaceable, safe, or at least as safe as a frontier establishment could be. Not that that meant too much. There were still roaming gunmen, overly brave youth thinking they could be the next great bank robbers. Sometimes even just senseless violence.

Jeb shuddered involuntarily. The senseless violence was the worst. No rhyme or reason. No ability to protect or guard against it. Out of the darkness and back to whence it had come. It was what had brought Jeb to the town in the first place. He'd been happy once, content. It seemed like a past life when he thought back on the ranch outside of Dallas. He'd had his land, his wife, his children. He'd worked hard and taken care of those close to him. But none of that mattered when a gang came out of the east, targeting Jeb for no reason anyone could ever pin down, other than he was conveniently on their path. He'd been out on the range that day, oblivious until he'd been hailed down in the late afternoon by a neighbor bearing the news of the grisly scene at his home.

That had almost broken him. Everything he'd loved, everything he'd worked for, the only people important to him, murdered, because he hadn't been there. *It wouldn't have mattered; you'd've been dead, too.* That was the solace the local sheriff had tried to give him. But in that moment, Jeb didn't want solace. He didn't want peace. He wanted revenge. He wanted justice. That was the day something inside him broke, a part of him that he didn't believe could be fixed. And most days, he didn't care to fix it.

He tracked the men to Amarillo, coming on the scene moments too late again. The group of hooligans had met their match the day before Jeb had arrived, and while he thought he would feel relief, some kind of pleasure in seeing that righteousness had worked things out in its own way, he'd simply felt empty. His was to be the hand that brought them down, not another random act of violence by men who knew nothing and cared less about whom they shot. At a loss, but needing something to keep him satiating his need for justice, Jeb had signed on as a deputy that day and worked his way up in the intervening years.

He stood in Richard's living room, regaining his bearings after the slight trip back in time. Was that what was motivating him? His own need for the world to make sense and be right, in spite of the fact that it never seemed to be? He took off his hat and ran a hand through his hair. There had to be some logic in all this. If it had been random, like Jeb's family, there wouldn't have been a message. He couldn't stop coming back to that.

Jeb looked around the room, satisfied with the thoroughness of his search on the first floor and, while he was not hopeful in his upstairs pursuit, he had no choice left but to go through the untouched rooms again. Perhaps in the heat of the moment, the men had taken off without what they'd been looking for. That could be why they'd holed up in the cabin so close by; they were waiting for things to cool down before coming back and getting what they'd sought. If that were the case, there was still a chance.

Jeb walked up the stairs and into Richard and Shae's room. He supposed a clever man might hide something in the room of his children, but for all Richard's faults, stingy, stubborn, greedy, he wasn't a bad man. Hiding something around Benjamin or Daisy would only endanger the children. And while it would seem logical to assume Richard wouldn't want to put Shae at risk either — though he clearly had, somehow — Jeb figured Richard would be the type to keep anything important either away from everyone, or very near his person. Richard wasn't untrustworthy, per se, but he certainly was selective in those he decided to trust.

Feeling he was on the right track, Jeb went straight to Richard's side of the room, searching through the sparse personal items that still sat where Richard had left them. Then, in the back of a bureau drawer, Jeb found what he was looking for. Tucked away out of sight, a beaten, leather day book had been jammed in the corner of the drawer. Jeb turned to the last few entries, his eyes scanning the pages quickly.

He had it. And he needed to move fast. Running down the steps, leaving the door to the home open, Jeb jumped on the Appaloosa and raced back to the sheriff's office, hoping Aaron would've returned from his trip by the time Jeb got there.

***

About thirty minutes after Jeb's return, thirty long minutes filled with pacing and cursing under his breath, Aaron stepped into the office. The man looked as if he had news as well, but Jeb had held up a hand before Aaron could get too far into his tale.

"I bet at least half of your story's in here," Jeb had said, handing the book to Aaron. The deputy sat down in the extra chair without a word and began to read.

Jeb continued pacing while Aaron's sighs and muttered exclamations of surprise became more frequent and intense. *How could Richard have done this?* Jeb kept wondering. *How could he have risked his family, his children?*

Surely Shae couldn't have known. Surely she would've said something by now. Her name was nowhere to be found in the book, which in a way, Jeb supposed, was a relief. Otherwise, it would mean the woman had been lying to him the entire time she'd been in his home. And in a way that was equally concerned to Jeb, it would mean that he'd fallen for it.

"Dovetails," Aaron said finally. "It fits perfectly with what I've been hearing. Amazing."

"Amazing ..." Jeb sighed. "I don't know if that's the precise word I'd be using, but it's something."

The book, now resting on Aaron's knee, has been part ledger, part detailed instructions. But as a whole, it was a perfectly painted picture of Richard's involvement in the illegal sale of guns and moonshine to a variety of patrons in the town and surrounding area, reaching out into places Jeb never knew Richard had even been. And one name was repeated more than any other: Vanderheist.

"He was doing this right under our noses," Aaron said. "I mean, I know everybody's got their flaws, but this man was crooked as an old dog's leg. If I hadn't seen it in his own hand, I don't know if I'da believed it."

Jeb nodded. "Which tells us a number of things. One, there must be money involved. Either Richard hid it, which I'm starting to see as less and less likely. If there was money, we'd've known. A man can't hide it long, especially not a man like Richard. Greedy as he was, he still would've wanted more. He'd've bought land, I almost guarantee it. Something valuable but not immediately expendable."

Aaron flipped back a page in the book and ran his finger down a line of columns. "You're right," he said. "At least partially. There was money involved, but it looks like it was a lack of it that was the problem."

"That was my impression as well," Jeb said. "So, you think the whole thing was just a message, not to Richard, but to the rest of this Vanderheist's men? A way to let word spread that you don't cross the man, or else?"

Aaron looked up at the ceiling. "As much as I want it to be something else, it sure looks that way."

"What did you hear out with the tribe?" Jeb asked. "I don't wanna sling mud, but some of the names in there ain't exactly white."

"Yeah," Aaron said. "Like I said, this Dovetails is right up with it."

"All right," Jeb said. "I'm gonna need you to get me out there."

Aaron sat for a moment. Jeb knew the native men had always tolerated Aaron, had taken him in, but their hospitality beyond that was often unclear. They were a proud people, preferring to live life as much removed from the white plague as they could. But, he mused, this was different.

"I don't see that they have much choice," Aaron said finally. "We all got a problem and it comes from the same man." He glanced out the window at the afternoon sky. "You wanna go now?"

"No," Jeb said, walking around the desk and finally sitting down. "Tomorrow will do. Tonight we need to get that book straightened out. I'm not getting duped by anyone again."

Aaron leaned forward and sat the book between them on the desk. "Let's get started."

Chapter Seven

At the same time, Shae stood in the kitchen of Jeb's home, diligently working to prepare the evening meal, though thanks to the presence of Grace, Shae found herself wiping tears of laughter from her eyes much more frequently than the chopping of the onions in front of her would've required. The woman had a golden tongue and despite the fact Shae knew Grace's stories were likely more than a little embellished, the neighbor had been a more than welcome addition to her life on this side of Amarillo.

Grace had an easy demeanor that belied a deeper understanding. Shae could feel it in the way the woman spoke. Every story was intentionally entertaining, not for the sake of itself, but to guide Shae back toward happiness, back toward some kind of normalcy. If the truth was bent, or in some instances more likely broken, well, it was two people trying to share joy. The truth had been twisted up for worse reasons than that.

"I could get used to having you around," Grace said, taking a piece of one of the onions and popping it into her mouth. "The rest of the girls this side are getting tired of hearing the same jokes."

"Ah, so that's it," Shae laughed. "You just needed a new audience."

Grace shrugged and smiled, stopping to allow Daisy a moment of her attention before taking a seat in one of the empty chairs by the table. Benjamin sat next to her, a slate board covered with chalk lines and squiggles in front of him.

"You could use an extra set of hands, too," Grace said. "You got a lot on you right now."

"Oh, is that it?" Shae grinned. "You're just here out of the goodness of your heart?"

"I really am quite the saint, aren't I?" Grace laughed.

"You're something," Shae replied.

Grace plugged the chalk from Benjamin's hand and in large letters wrote "B E N" at the top of the slate. "Practice those and your momma's gonna be so impressed," she whispered to the boy. Grace sat quietly for a moment, drawing Shae's look.

"Okay," Shae said. "What's on your mind? This is the quietest you've been since we met."

Grace smiled. "My husband wouldn't believe it if you told him. He doesn't think I know the meaning of the word. Says I even talk in my sleep."

"That I believe," Shae said, brushing the chopped onion from the cutting board into a wooden bowl.

"Well, thing is," Grace said, "and I know I'm overstepping my bounds here, but it don't do to have too much hemming and hawing out here."

Shae looked at the woman.

"I know that sounds a little silly coming from me," Grace said, her tone light but with undertones of something more sincere. "But the fact is, there's a certain way of life here, and it takes a strong woman to keep up with it. I'm sorry for your loss, I truly am. I can't — don't want to — imagine what kind of things you must be going through. And I'm deeply sorry if I'm talking out of line here; you just say the word and I'll not mention it again."

"No," Shae said, anticipating the woman's train of thought. To be honest, the last few nights, Shae had been thinking along the same lines. But the guilt she'd felt, the idea of even considering some of these things, had made her lock the thoughts deep in her mind. It felt wrong, somehow, untrue. Like she was sullying Richard's memory.

"So, I'm not terribly off the mark to say you've had passing thoughts," Grace said gently.

Shae set the knife down on the counter, looking down at her hands. "It feels wrong to say so."

Grace moved over to stand beside her, putting a hand on the woman's shoulder. "It may feel that way, but it doesn't mean it's true. You know where you stand, you know where you're trying to bring these kids up. Maybe it feels like you're not doing something right, but facts don't care much for feelings, more often than not. And out here the facts are pretty cold. You got two wonderful children there and you're gonna need some help raising them. You know you can count on me, but I got a family of my own as well. We need to be thinking about your next steps."

"It's just so soon," Shae said, looking over at the woman. "Don't you see? Richard is barely gone and now I have to start looking for another suitor? I never planned on doing that in my life. A week ago I was happy, at home, with my family. Now I'm out here trying to make heads or tails of something I never even considered happening."

"I know, dear," Grace said softly. "I know. And I can't start to say I understand what you're going through. But, as the men so love to say, 'that's the way of the west.' I wonder sometimes if they really know what they mean when they say that. Seems to me it's us womenfolk who take the real brunt of the trouble out here, trying to keep a home, raise a decent family, all the while dealing with the danger and the dirt and" — she fanned herself, a ghost of a grin at the corners of her mouth — "the heat! Lordy. When Calvin said we were fixing to move out west, I admit I was hoping for something a little farther north."

Shae grinned in spite of herself. The woman had a skill. Grace could dance around an issue, lightly stepping in to make a point before deftly skipping away again, gingerly easing ideas into Shae's mind that the woman herself was afraid to admit.

"The way I see it," Grace said, "and again, this is just one woman speaking here, and as your friend, but the way I see it, you seem pretty at home right here where you stand. You aren't going to find a man as reliable and honorable as Jebediah Barnet. And I'd say that in front of Calvin, too," she laughed. "And all that aside, you've known the man a long time, long as any, I'd imagine."

"That's true," Shae said, wanting to admit to the mere basic facts without having to commit herself to a confession of the feelings she'd been noticing in herself. Seeing Jeb come home in the evening, being there in the morning when he left for work. There was a comfort in the routine, at least that's what she'd told herself. It was simply her mind trying to find some kind of regularity after the chaos. But if she was honest, more than once she'd felt the flutter of a butterfly in her stomach in the man's presence.

"But, still," Shae continued. "Already? It seems disrespectful."

"I know," Grace said. "But you have to ask yourself, what is more disrespectful, trying to keep your family safe and happy, or shirking your duty as a mother and a woman because of something you can't change?"

"Grace —" Shae shuddered at the memories of that night. "Duty is one thing, but I don't know that a man would want me anymore. I've been ... violated. I've been exposed. Aaron,

Jeb, they walked in and saw, well, frankly, I don't even know. I don't remember. I don't want to remember. But I've been dirtied by all this. And even if I hadn't, what man would want to raise another's children?"

Grace took Shae's hands in her own. "Dear, I'm not saying you have to propose to Jeb when he gets home. Though *that* would be a story to tell, so if you do, don't you go finding out from someone else," she said, with a smile. "All I'm saying is, when you have a moment during the day, or when you lay down at night, you think about where you are. Not as Richard Tulley's widow, but as a woman with a job to do. And don't you go pigeonholing Jeb either. He's not like the other men you've known, not by a long shot."

***

The next day, Jeb and Aaron sat in the shade of a small grove of trees somewhere between Amarillo and the border of the New Mexico Territory. They'd left early, before the sun had fully risen, in order to meet with the Comanche chief before the tribe had moved any farther westward. In the background, men and women prepared for the journey, having only been halted by the arrival of the lawmen so early in the day.

The dark-skinned man sat across from the two, his storied silence in full evidence. Jeb knew this was mostly due to his own presence, but with the situation at hand, he didn't want to send Aaron out on his own. If things were going to be happening between the tribe and the law in Amarillo, Jeb wanted to ensure that the chief understood it was coming from him, and that he was a man the chief could trust.

They'd met, briefly, on occasion in their youth. Aaron had convinced the natives to allow Jeb's presence for a few festivals, but as the two had grown, it had been no secret that Aaron would always possess a welcome that was not extended to any of the other settlers in the area. Not for the first time, Jeb wondered just what it was that set his deputy apart so with such distinction. Then again, he thought, it didn't do to look a gift horse in the mouth, and for the moment, he was more than thankful to have Aaron along. The chief showed little interest in talking to the sheriff.

"The problems in your town are none of our concern," the chief had told him again and again. "We've done our best to avoid you. You continue to move onto our land and we continue to move away from you. You refuse to understand the message we are sending you and we tire of this willful ignorance. The lawlessness you deal with is the lawlessness born of your kind. Don't bring your troubles to my people."

Jeb glanced at Aaron. "In this instance," Jeb said, "I think our troubles might be the same. Perhaps it started with our people, though I give you my word that the man we are after is no friend of mine."

The chief seemed unmoved by the statement. No friend of Jeb's was probably also unlikely to be a friend of the Comanche, but the tribe had consistently kept itself as distant as possible from the townspeople.

"He murdered one of my deputies," Jeb continued. "Dishonored the man's wife. And we think he might be involved with the tribes as well."

The chief's face grew grim, though Jeb was unsure if it was at the acts of Vanderheist's men or perhaps a misunderstanding about how Jeb was implying the man was 'involved.'

"Your people know little of honor," the chief said.

Jeb gritted his teeth. Now wasn't the time for argument. And, given what the man had seen in his life, Jeb couldn't blame him for the statement. "This man knows even less,"

Jeb said. "I don't have all the answers yet, but Aaron tells me you've had some kind of interactions with him as well. All I want to do is ensure we are in communication. You can see farther than I can. You hear more than I hear. What's happening in Amarillo isn't only happening there. If we're going to find Vanderheist—"

The chief stood abruptly. "No!" he cried out. "We will have nothing to do with this man. He's the reason we're moving west. Too many times has this white devil been the cause of strife amongst my people."

Jeb knew it was a risky statement, but he felt he was about to lose the man anyway, so he spoke clearly. "And what will you do when he follows you to the New Mexico Territory? Move again?"

"If we must," the chief said. "Your kind have chased us across this land since before my father. We stay and fight, you murder us. We move on, you still hunt us down. I'm tired of the bloodshed."

Jeb stood to look the man in the eye. He wanted the chief to see his respect, his determination, not just another white man attempting to talk the natives into a shady deal. "I will handle the bloodshed."

The chief looked between Jeb and Aaron, seeming to consider the boldness of the sheriff. After a moment, he sat again. "This man," the chief said. "He brings guns, whiskey, problems. Some of my people, they welcome him. I've dealt with this long enough. I will not tolerate the chaos he has caused. But you say we can bring an end to it, then I am willing to assist you. Provided," he paused, "he is dealt with in a final manner. We will not allow him among us again. If we see him" — the chief turned to Aaron — "we will not allow any of you among us again."

For the first time since their arrival, Aaron spoke. "I give you my word."

The chief looked from Aaron to Jeb. "Soon," he said, "soon he will return. At the beginning of each month, he comes to make his deals, sell his wares. It's then that you can know where to find him."

Chapter Eight

That evening, after a late dinner, Jeb sat at the table with Shae and the kids. It had been funny coming home to them, in a way. Benjamin had run out the door, excited, leaping up toward Jeb without a doubt in his mind that the man would catch him. His muscles remembering the movements so well, Jeb deftly caught the boy and spun him up and around so he was sitting on Jeb's shoulders. Amid laughter, Jeb carried the child inside, remembering to stoop low through the doorway and then, equally smoothly, tipping Benjamin frontwards over his shoulder, catching him, and spinning him into a chair at the dining table.

The boy's laughter was infectious. Shae smiled behind a hand and even Daisy giggled away happily from her bassinet, gleefully without understanding other than that there was joy in the room. Jeb had removed his hat and plunked it on the boy, sitting down beside him at the table.

The man looked around him, realizing for a moment how familiar and yet how strange the preceding minutes had been. How many years had it been since he'd done just that, those same motions, but at a house miles away, a lifetime away? He looked around the room, happy to have people in his life like this again, but also feeling the pangs of remorse that reminded him these were not his people. This wasn't his son. This wasn't the woman he so desperately wanted to see just one more time.

Shae, as if sensing his unease, had hurriedly gotten the food on the table, picking up a line of banter and neighborhood gossip that Jeb knew could've come from nothing other than time with Mrs. Grace Allen. He smiled at the thought. The neighbor woman had been the first he'd gotten in touch with the morning after Shae had come to stay with him. He hadn't erred in his choice.

Benjamin had kept up his usual stream of questions; Daisy had caused her typical havoc reaching for anything she could. And Shae had sat across from him, a hint of a contented smile on her lips as, from what Jeb could tell, she moved through the familiar motions of family life precisely as he had done moments before.

***

That evening, after the children had been put to bed, Jeb sat out on the front porch, his feet up on the railing, his body weary from the long day's ride out to the Comanche tribe and back. The hours in the saddle wore on him like they hadn't ten years ago, and though he was still a young man, he missed the days when he rarely got out more than a few miles from his home.

Shae came out to join him as the inside of the house settled down for the night, two glasses of iced tea in her hands. Despite the temperatures the days often reached, the evenings had remained cool, adding to the peacefulness Jeb wanted to soak in while he had a few moments to do so.

"Thank you," he said as Shae handed him a glass. "That was quite the meal you served up this evening, as well. You're going to spoil me."

The woman smiled demurely and Jeb wondered if he hadn't hit the nail precisely on the head. He had wondered when this situation would alter. The first few days had been so hectic, so much chaos and emotion both over the case and in the home as two acquaintances began to adapt to the daily rhythms of one another. Two families suddenly pushed together.

Could he still consider himself that way, though? He'd been a bachelor for so long, and yet, the routine of his home and life had changed only as much as was necessitated by the move and the singleness of his existence. Not six months ago he'd caught himself wanting to set places for everyone at dinner, instead of just the one plate he needed.

"Grace Allen came by today," Shae said, bringing Jeb out of his reverie.

"Did she?" he said. "She's a firecracker, that one."

Shae laughed. "That she is, but I wanted to say thank you."

He glanced over at her.

"I assume you had something to do with it," Shae said. "I know, or at least I'm learning, that Grace probably hasn't ever met a stranger, but I get the distinct feeling it wasn't by chance she's been stopping in to chat, sometimes more than once a day."

Jeb smiled. "I may've mentioned something about you being here on your own, but it wasn't nothing ..." he trailed off, unsure how to address the exact situation that he had been concerned about when he'd first gone to see Grace.

"I understand," Shae said. "And whether it was precisely about what happened to Richard and me, or whether it was just you being thoughtful, I still wanted you to know I appreciate it very much. Those first few days were ... dark."

Jeb watched as she took a drink of her tea, looking out into the night and avoiding his gaze.

"I ..." Jeb started, unsure if, or how, he wanted to express the broken past that they both shared. He'd kept mostly to himself since he'd been in Amarillo. It wasn't that he had purposefully kept what happened to his family a secret, but it wasn't something he brought up either. The men in the station were aware; he was sure word had spread somewhat.

He didn't know how much Richard may or may not have shared, though. And besides, what had happened to Shae wasn't precisely like what Jeb had gone through. Though, he mused, maybe alike enough.

"I just want you to know you're welcome here, long as you want," he finished lamely.

There was the briefest of pauses where Jeb could tell the woman was debating within herself. He'd been around enough people in his days as sheriff to learn how to read silences. Sometimes it was because a person was trying to concoct a lie. Other times it was because they were trying to figure out how exactly to tell the truth. Shae seemed to be struggling with whether she wanted to speak at all. Unsure if he wanted to continue the conversation any further down the route he supposed it was about to take, Jeb let the woman work it out on her own.

Finally, after another nip at her drink, Shae spoke up. "Grace and I were talking today," she said, then paused again. "Well, that's not fair. I can't necessarily pin this on Grace, though I suppose she did allow me the time to talk and think aloud."

Jeb looked out into the night, giving the woman her time.

"You see," Shae said, "the west is a hard place to survive …" She took a hurried sip of her drink. "No, that's not what I mean." She sat her glass down on the wooden planks beside her, folding her hands in her lap. She looked over at Jeb.

The man sighed, not in exasperation, but in resolve to continue moving forward, to keep dealing the hands dealt him. Maybe even to see the silver lining in things. This was a good woman beside him. A solid, reliable young lady who had proven herself as a mother, as a homemaker, and most importantly, as someone strong enough to be the wife of a lawman. And she, more than anyone, knew how much that could entail.

"Shae," Jeb started, "I think I can imagine where the conversation went between you and Mrs. Allen. I suppose my question would be, where do you come down on it? I assume you don't find the idea downright off-putting, or you wouldn't have mentioned it in the first place. But you also don't seem completely sure of how you feel."

"Yes," Shae said, looking down, "I suppose that would be an accurate way to describe my thoughts. There has just been so much going on. With Richard, with," she hesitated, "my experience. But that doesn't give me the right to give up on the children. They need their mother, even more now that I'm the only parent they have, and regardless of what I think or feel, I need to have them at the forefront of my mind."

Jeb nodded. "That is one way to look at it. An admirable way," he said. "But I'd counter with this: a momma who hasn't figured herself out ain't much good to her younguns either. You gotta know what it is you want, not just jump at something because it's there."

Shae grew silent again and Jeb almost kicked himself for the choice of words. He sounded as if he were admonishing the woman rather than trying to encourage her, be on her side.

"Look," he tried again. "I've heard the term 'marriage of convenience' just as many times as you have, believe it or not." The woman looked over at him, surprised. Apparently, Richard, whoever the man had been, had at least kept Jeb's story to himself. Jeb sighed. "I was married before as well," Jeb said. "I grew up not far from here, of course, that's how I knew Aaron and some of the townsfolk and what have you. But, around twenty, I got me a wife and a farm over Dallas way. Had us a good little family there. A good life." He paused, letting the memories come back. Sometimes it hurt, but sometimes it did him good to remember that there was a time in his life he'd been truly happy.

"But ..." Shae broke his chain of thought.

"But," Jeb said, settling back into his chair, "things happened. You know about that as well as anyone, I'd say. I'm not gonna sit here and tell you I understand what you're going through, but I'll tell you ... well ... I'll tell you I understand what it's like to lose your family." He had to be careful. His emotions were always unpredictable when it came to his past. Sometimes depressing, sometimes melancholic, but sometimes angry. And there was no one left to vent that anger on who deserved it. He thought seeing the men who'd done it in the ground would grant him some kind of peace, but he'd learned, after many a long night, there wasn't likely to be any peace coming his way.

"I'm sorry," Shae said.

"Oh," Jeb sighed. "It ain't your fault." He took a drink from his glass, more for something to do with his shaking hands than to quench a thirst.

"No," Shae said. "I'm sorry for being here. I'm sorry for what I've been doing. It must be so difficult for you to have another woman in your home now. I never intended to take your wife's place. Jeb, if I'd known this sooner, I would've never thought of bringing myself and the children here."

Jeb looked over at her, surprised. He'd heard "I'm sorry" and "my condolences" so many times the words had lost all meaning to him. But this was different. Shae wasn't expressing a trite, emotionless pleasantry, the woman was seeing into his life, grasping things he felt that even he hadn't been able to put into words.

"First thing in the morning I'll try and find us another place," Shae said. "I understand why you didn't want to share this with me, but I'm so, so sorry for the pain I must've been causing you."

Jeb watched her for a moment. Finally, he spoke. "I'll be ..."

Shae looked at him, unsure of how to interpret his words.

"I just ..." Jeb took a moment, trying to figure out how to express himself. "I didn't expect you to say that, is all. And, well, I appreciate it, Shae. I really do. Not because you've been any kind of inconvenience. Shoot, I wouldn'ta let you stay anywhere else even if you'd asked. But, well, just thank you, I guess."

"You're welcome," she said hesitantly.

"Listen, though," Jeb said. "I need you to know something now. You ain't done nothing wrong being here. You haven't hurt me. You haven't taken anyone's place. If I'm being honest, and maybe I shoulda been before now, but if I'm telling you the truth, I've been happier having you all here than I have in a long time. You bring some life back into this place."

Shae laughed quietly. "We certainly know how to do that. I can't imagine what it must be like for you. All this time you've lived on your own and now there's a woman and not just a little boy, but a baby even, bursting into your home."

Jeb smiled. "Ah, it's been good having the boy around. Reminds me of my own. Always wanting to know why, why, why. He's a smart little whip, you got there."

"Oh, he just loves you," the woman said. "It might be why, why, why for you but it's when, when, when for me. When will Jeb be home? When's Jeb coming back? When can I see the sheriff? You're quite the hero in his eyes."

Jeb laughed. "He'll grow out of that soon enough."

"I don't know," the woman said. "I'm inclined to agree with him."

Jeb could feel the spark between them. If there had been a moment to kiss this woman, something he never expected to find himself thinking, then this was it. He looked over at her, the moonlight glowing in her hair, her eyes sparkling in the dark.

But, no. He couldn't. Not yet. Maybe everyone else would laugh if he said it was too soon, but there was no other way to put it. Even if it wasn't too soon for Shae, it felt too soon for Jeb. The years had gone by, but he still felt that longing for his wife. It would still feel like a betrayal.

"Well, about that," he said, trying to change the subject smoothly, but judging by the look of disappointment on Shae's face, having no success whatsoever, "I wanted to let you know it looks like we might be making some progress on things finally."

"Oh?" the woman was interested, of course. But he could tell by her tone this was in no way the conversation she wanted to be having.

"Yeah," he said, looking back out over the porch railing. "Seems the fellers who come by your way are just the beginning. We've got some names outta them. Aaron and me been over to talk to the tribe, get their take on things, and I think we're coming close to being able to make a move."

"That's good," Shae said quietly.

"It is," the man mused. "If I had the choice, I'd just go out and round 'em all up myself. As soon as I do that though, they're out walking again by sun-up the next morning. The feller we're looking at has some deep pockets on him. But I think if we play our cards right, we can dig a hole for him even deeper. Put him away for a long time."

"I'm glad to hear that," Shae said, reaching over to get her glass from the porch.

"Look," Jeb started, wanting to set things right before the evening ended. Shae, however, had no intention of doing so.

"I understand," she said. "And you're right. This is what you need to be focusing on right now. Let me tell you this, Jebediah. I am not upset with you at all for handling this situation the way you are. You're a lawman. I understand what that means to you. I will simply say, when you are ready to discuss matters of a more personal nature, well, I will be waiting."

Shae walked over and plucked the empty glass from his hand, surprisingly, a smile still on her face. "Good night, sir."

"Good night, Shae," he said, watching her walk back inside and then turning his eyes out again to the dark night sky.

Chapter Nine

The next day passed slowly for Jeb. Aaron had gone out to track down some of the names in Richard's ledger pages and Jeb had begun the slow process of finding a replacement for his murdered deputy. Amarillo wasn't a small town, and there was no shortage of men, young men especially, fired up by the idea of pinning on a star and sauntering through town with a gun on their hip. The problem was, after the violence against the Tulley family, the men approaching Jeb were of the fiery-tempered sort. It was an attitude that could at times be useful, but as a general rule caused more problems than it was worth.

On the other side of things, the men Jeb had in mind were level-headed enough to see trouble in the situation and think twice before placing themselves in the thick of it. It wasn't that they were cowardly. Far from it. It was that the men had families of their own, that they understood the risk they were taking by signing on with the sheriff. If push came to shove, Jeb knew he could count on the men to come out of the woodwork. Amarillo was a town of good citizens and the main reason for that was their own desire to keep the city that way. But at the end of the day, if trouble could be avoided, most folks chose to do so. And Jeb couldn't blame them a bit for it. After all, he hadn't gotten his star until he'd had nothing left to lose.

Toward the end of the day, Aaron had stopped back in, given Jeb a next-to-useless report on a very uneventful day of riding and asking questions, and headed back to his own home for the night. On a whim, as he prepared to leave himself, Jeb grabbed Richard's diary, ostensibly to look for more information in the case. But if he were honest with himself, he was no less curious than any other person might've been. There were secrets in this book, and if Jeb was going to be involved in the man's life, in any way, he wanted to have all the information he could.

After dinner that evening, Jeb had gone out onto the porch, as was becoming his habit at the end of the day. It wasn't to avoid Shae and the kids in any way, but a part of him thought the bedtime ritual was a private thing and he didn't have any intention of pushing his way into a situation he didn't belong in. Of course, it wasn't due to a lack of request on Benjamin's part. But the boy had been appeased with a general good night to the trio before they'd gone upstairs. Whether Ben had any idea his mother came back down afterward was anyone's guess, but Jeb tried to keep the thoughts far from his mind when he could.

He opened the book at random, flipping through the pages he was already familiar with. The lists of numbers carefully written in, the names beside each. Some looked to be delivery schedules, payment dates. This was the information Aaron had been working from and, while Jeb was familiar with it, it wasn't where his curiosity lay that evening.

Instead, he turned to the other pages, the blocks of texts written in Richard's large, though legible hand, scrawled across the pages as the mood seemed to take him. There was no set pattern to the entries. Some came between other, more business-related entries. Some went on for page after page. Others were short paragraphs or lines scratched out in a moment's time.

As Jeb looked through them at random, hoping for something substantial, he did notice one name that kept reappearing almost as much as Vanderheist's.

Rebekah.

At first, Jeb assumed that the woman must have something to do with the alcohol and guns; why else would she turn out so many times in a book dedicated to hardly anything else? If Vanderheist had a partner, it wouldn't surprise Jeb in any way. The sheer size of the operation seemed to grow as he and Aaron looked further into it. And a female accomplice wouldn't be outlandish. Often, the women could be more ruthless than the men, at least in Jeb's experience.

But something was tugging at him. The meetings with Rebekah, while not nearly as regulated as those with Vanderheist or the other men involved, still happened in an almost scheduled fashion, as if the rule had been something looser, like "once a week" rather than the set-in-stone dates noted for meetings with Vanderheist.

After a moment, it dawned on Jeb.

This wasn't just a journal of Richard's work with Vanderheist. It wasn't purely an emotionless volume at all. Slipped in between the entries that no doubt marked moments of violence and lawlessness, these were the notations of a man involved with a woman. Jeb balked at using the term "love"; Richard was married already. But infatuation, lust perhaps, yes. Those were both evident in the man's meticulous records. It read almost like a conquest, notes on the adventure that Richard had arrogantly written to remind himself of his clever movements, his smooth lies, his success in pulling the wool over not only Jeb's eyes with his illicit activities involving Vanderheist, but over Shae's eyes in his illicit activities with Rebekah.

Jeb began to read closer, astonished at the duplicity of the man, not just as a deputy, but as a husband, as a person. The entries, though not all dated, went back at least a year, simply based on when the book began because no sooner was Vanderheist on the scene than Rebekah was making her appearances. Jeb wondered, and flipped back to the first few pages. Indeed, there it was. Vanderheist wasn't even mentioned until five or ten leaves in.

The audacity of the man astounded him. A record book for a business was understandable, whether or not it was legal. In some ways, Jeb supposed, it was almost a necessary risk when there were no banks involved, no official ways to keep track of payments and debts. But this book had begun its life purely as a testament to this Rebekah woman. And he'd kept it in his home, the very bedroom he shared with his wife.

Jeb began to flip through the pages faster, searching for a surname. The name Rebekah wasn't uncommon, if the spelling happened to be. Perhaps Richard hadn't been mistaken, but, as Jeb knew, Richard was an intelligent man. Much more than he'd given him credit for, he was coming to believe. And one didn't trifle with love, obsession, whatever the proper term was. Surely the -kah was correct. The problem was that Jeb knew plenty of Rebeccas, Rebecas, Rebekas. For all he knew, this woman may have been one of them and he'd just assumed a spelling when he'd heard the name.

As Jeb was running through the list of women he knew and who also would've had occasion to cross Richard's path — and as lawmen the list was growing long — he heard Shae come across the room behind him. Hurriedly, he closed the book, tossing it on the porch beside him. The last thing this woman needed was to know of her useless husband's infidelity. That would just be another thing Jeb would take care of for her. He glanced up as she came out.

"Beautiful night," Shae said, sitting down beside him.

Chapter Ten

Vanderheist stood in his office the next day, not terribly far from where Jeb sat behind the sheriff's desk. The German had become adept at hiding in plain sight, at least when it came to his places of business. The little office in Amarillo wasn't his favorite, but it was a good station from which to conduct the affairs necessary for the hub of his business in that area.

Behind him, in a plush velvet chair across the desk, sat Trevor, yet again having unfortunate news for the boss, but at least having had the propriety to have gathered it at Vanderheist's own request this time.

The occurrence at the Tulley homestead had been a disaster from start to finish; Vanderheist was learning more and more about it every day. While the ledger the deputy had kept was largely irrelevant — Vanderheist had his own set of much more accurate and detailed books — the fact that the volume remained unaccounted for was something that could come back to haunt him.

Not only that, but the family of the deputy left question marks Vanderheist didn't like to consider. The children would have to be dealt with one way or another. But there were orphans all over the territories finding new homes daily. And Vanderheist wasn't cold enough to consider a four-year-old and an infant a threat to his business. The wife, however, caused him more than a little concern. Women were always so unpredictable. The wives of sheriffs and deputies were often the worst. It was as if the city gave them a star the same time it did their husbands. And if it wasn't that, it was some noble hero coming in to save the family in despair.

No, Vanderheist had no time for any of this. And so, he'd sent his loyal dog Trevor out to gather some information.

After all, the man might be too cowardly to pull the trigger when needed, but he'd proven himself more than adept at watching things happen, and sometimes that skill was even more valuable.

"From what I seen," Trevor was saying, "she's been there for a while. I tried to talk to the neighbor lady about it, but she wasn't having none of it. Told me to mind my own concern and slammed the door in my face."

"And who might this have been?" Vanderheist asked from his place by the window.

"Aw, I didn't get her name or nothing. Just some gal I seen coming back from there. Figured she'd know as much as anybody else."

"Well, I suppose this isn't a wholly unforeseen turn of events," Vanderheist mused. "It makes a certain amount of sense. It is unfortunate, however, for the former Mrs. Tulley, at least, that she didn't have any family in the area. She's already gone through so much."

Trevor snickered from his chair, earning him a glare from Vanderheist that set the lackey aback.

"I take no joy in being what some may call evil," Vanderheist said to the man. "I merely do what needs to be done in order to succeed. What is the phrase you have here? You must break a few eggs?"

Trevor nodded.

"Well, eggs must be broken, and while it is unfortunate the eggs seem to always be Shae Tulley's, I'm afraid the situation can't be helped. If the sheriff insists on continuing to mettle with my concerns, then we're going to need to be rid of him sooner rather than later."

"And there's the boys," Trevor said.

"Very true," Vanderheist said. "It's more than difficult to run a bootlegging branch of our business when there's no one manning the stills." He turned back to the glass, pondering the situation for a moment.

"I can get rid of the sheriff easy enough," Trevor said boldly from behind him.

"Forgive me if I say I highly doubt that," Vanderheist replied. "Perhaps you could bumble your way through something, but you're already showing the lack of foresight that will undoubtedly be your undoing at some point. Most likely not terribly long from now, I'm sorry to say."

"What's to think about it?" Trevor asked. "I get the jump on him and he goes down just like any other feller with a bullet in the back."

Vanderheist's lip curled in distaste. "And then?" he prompted.

"Then? Well, then we get back to doing what we's doing. Nothing to it."

"You don't suppose the other deputy would have anything to say about your bold move?"

"Aw, shoot," Trevor said. Then after a moment, "Well, I'd just do the same to him. Two bullets don't cost much." He grinned at his bravado.

"I suppose I will take that into consideration," Vanderheist said. "But for now, let's try and think slightly outside the box, shall we? We have a sheriff we need rather desperately to be rid of; we have a deputy's widow who unfortunately can't be trusted. And perhaps in a stroke of luck, we have them in the same household. Surely we can use this to our advantage."

Trevor just shrugged, crossing one leg over the other. "You just tell me what to do, boss. You're the brains here."

"So good of you to finally admit that," Vanderheist said sarcastically. "You've been out to the house now a handful of times. I would have to assume a man of your," he paused, "appearance could perhaps draw more attention than I'd really like. Unfortunately, you've also gotten the best lay of the land, as you say. This is what I'd like you to do," Vanderheist paused, looking at the man for a moment. "You can write, correct?"

For a moment Trevor attempted to look offended, then, almost blushing, muttered his answer. "I got mosta the letters, yeah."

"Numbers? You must be able to tell time."

"Well, yeah," Trevor said, growing more confident in this area. "How else you think I ever get where I'm going?"

"I often wonder," Vanderheist said quietly. "Nevertheless, here's what I need you to do. Return to the sheriff's home for the next day or two. Stay out of sight. I cannot stress that enough. Do not make a spectacle of yourself. Do not interact with the people there. Do not sleep. Do not wander off."

"All right, all right," Trevor said. "That's a lotta do-nots, though. What do you want me to do?"

"I want you to merely watch," Vanderheist said. "I want you to keep your eye on everything that happens in that home. Here." He walked over to his desk and removed a small notebook from a drawer. He tossed it to Trevor, plucking a short pencil from a mug on the desktop. "Take these and note down every time anyone comes or goes. And I mean anyone, Trevor. Any face that appears more than once, you make a note of it. Any occurrence that happens more than once, you write that down. What we need are patterns. Reliable, straightforward patterns."

"You wanna take him out at his house?" Trevor said.

"No," Vanderheist smiled. "Not him, her."

"All right," Trevor said. "I reckon I can handle a woman."

"Not quite." The German smiled. "We will need the woman, certainly, but we're going to only borrow her, as it were. Once we have the woman, the sheriff will come to us."

"And then?"

"And then, Trevor, whatever we want. Shooting another lawman in this town would undoubtedly bring more trouble than it would be worth. But if we were out away from town, perhaps, if the sheriff happened to just vanish one day, well, then that would be something that was no one's fault. Accidents take place, people die, it's part of the danger of being alive. If one of those accidents comes about due to our diligent planning, then that will just have to be something we keep to ourselves."

"And if the deputy comes too ..." Trevor grinned.

"I suppose two accidents are as easy to arrange as one," Vanderheist said. "Now go. The sooner we get this straightened out, the sooner we get back to work."

Trevor jumped up, tucking the notebook and pencil in his back pocket. "You got it, boss."

Vanderheist watched the man exit, heard him clomping down the wooden steps. Every man had his value. At least, for a time.

Chapter Eleven

The next morning after breakfast, Jeb was kneeling next to Ben on the kitchen floor. Breakfast had been served and cleared and just before the man had headed out for the day, Ben had caught him at the door, a small toy clutched in the boy's hands. Jeb remembered the look on the child's face; he'd seen it a few time's on his own son. It was the first young attempt at bravery. Ben's lower lip quivered but he had resolved to keep his tears inside. Jeb had taken one look and led the youth into the kitchen, pulling out a chair for them to use as a workbench.

"Looks like your horse's got a bit of a hitch in her giddy-up," the man said, carefully taking the toy, and its parts from Ben.

The boy nodded, apparently still uncertain if he could speak without crying.

"Well, it happens to the best of us," Jeb smiled. "Let's see what we're working with here." He sat the parts out in front of him. The horse, a simple pull-behind model, had come untied from its string, and the platform it rode on, a simple four-wheeled piece of wood, was now one wheel shy.

"She must be a wild one." Jeb smiled. "Usually they just throw a shoe. Was she in a rodeo?"

The boy grinned a little, shaking his head.

"No? Hm ..." Jeb furrowed his brow. "Maybe a race?"

Ben smiled wider, nodding.

"She looks likes a racin' horse," Jeb said. "Probably fast as lightning."

At the table, Shae looked quietly from where she was mending some old curtains she'd found in a trunk upstairs.

"Let's see here," Jeb laid the pieces out in front of him. "First step to solvin' any problem is to figure out what we're working with." He arranged the parts on the chair. "We got our tether here; looks like she musta been buckin' to throw that one."

Ben laughed. "She's wild!"

"Wild?" Jeb asked, pulling his hands back. "Well I don't have any carrots. Can you keep her calm for me? We can't have her dartin' off on three wheels."

The boy laughed again. "Stay, Mabel," he directed.

"You keep an eye on ole Mabel," Jeb said and picked up the wheel. "Throwed her tether and throwed her wheel. Lucky for us I happen to be a wheel and tether expert." After examining the small wooden pieces for a moment he walked over to the kitchen, rummaged in a drawer, and returned with a box of matches.

Ben's eyes widened slightly.

"That's a good response," Jeb said, hunkering back down next to the youth. "These things ain't usually for playin', so best you just let me and your ma do any repairs. Just like you're doin'." He took out a pocket knife and snipped the end of a match, shaving it down to a few thin splinters. "But this wood part here, it's just what we need for fixin' up Miss Mabel's wheel. Here." He held the horse out to the boy, turning the platform so he could work the wheel and the small wedges back on to the axle. After a few slight adjustments, he nodded to Ben. "Give 'er a spin."

The boy turned the wheel on his side, watching the axle move within its wooden tube, both wheels turning in sync. "You fixed it!"

"Oh, not yet," Jeb said, his tone playfully serious. "You said this is a wild horse. Well, now she's got her wheels back but we ain't got no way to keep her under control. What do you think we oughtta do?"

Ben pointed to the string on the chair.

"Brilliant," Jeb said. "Can't many folks ride a horse without no way to lead it. At least not if they wanna get where they's goin'. Now you keep holding her steady like you're doin'. Sometimes they get antsy ..."

"Antsy and prancy," the boy said, laughing.

"You aren't-a kiddin'," Jeb said, running the thin string through a loop where the horse's bit would go. "We gotta be real slow and gentle with horses. They're big, but they get scared too."

"Skittish," Ben said.

Jeb laughed this time. "You got it. And a skittish horse makes everybody nervous. And you know what happens when you get nervous?"

Ben shook his head.

"Well, then the horse gets even more nervous. Then you're both nervous, and that just won't do."

"We're all skittish!" Ben laughed, looking at his mother. "I'm skittish. Mom's skittish!"

Jeb glanced at Shae, catching her smile. "Now that's something I ain't never seen," he said. "You're momma's the bravest woman I know."

Ben looked back at him, almost skeptical. "Really?"

"Really," Jeb said, tightening the knot on the string. "The day she gets skittish we better all just head for the hills."

Ben laughed again. "Well, I'm not skittish either," he proclaimed.

"Good man," Jeb patted the floor in front of him. "Let's see how ole Mabel feels now."

The boy sat the horse down and gave a few cautionary pulls, clearly afraid he was going to encounter the same type of accident that had so recently occurred. After a few passes at his feet, he lit up. "You fixed her!'

Before Jeb was prepared for it, Ben threw himself into the sheriff's arms. "Thank you!" The boy squeezed the man tight around the neck.

"Everybody has an accident once in a while," Jeb said, cautiously hugging the boy back. "You just come find me if you need some help. And what don't you do?"

"Play with the matches!" Ben yelled as he raced off out of the room, Mabel the horse clattering across the hard wooden floor behind him.

Jeb stood back up, looking over at Shae. He shrugged and said, "Maybe he'll remember?"

"I'm sure he will," she said, smiling. "Probably more than you realize."

Jeb cocked his head to the side, trying to ascertain just what the woman was implying.

"You're good with him, Jeb. I never saw his father do something like that one time."

"Ah," Jeb fidgeted with his belt, uncomfortable with the comment. "Richard ... he had a lot on his mind, I reckon."

"As do you," Shae said. "And I want to thank you for taking the time to help anyway."

"Well ..." Jeb trailed off, unsure what to say. He glanced outside, at the door. "I guess I oughtta be gettin'."

He took a few steps toward the door and then paused. *Skittish*, he thought to himself. Jeb squared his shoulders and turned back to face Shae. "Perhaps you heard, or, well, I'm sure you did, but the fair is coming on Sunday. And, ya see, well with Ben and all I thought maybe you all might like to get out and have a nice time. Change of scenery. Let the boy burn off some energy maybe."

Shae smiled. "Surely the sheriff isn't getting worn down by a four-year-old. Heaven help us."

Jeb started to protest then grinned in return. "Well, I just thought we might all enjoy going. If you want to, that is."

"I'd be honored," Shae said, "on one condition."

"What's that?"

"There's some fabric upstairs. It was with these old curtains and I didn't mean to pry, but, this house could use some tending to."

"Oh," Jeb said. "You go right ahead. Whatever you think we, or the house, needs." He felt his cheeks redden a bit.

"Well, if it's okay," Shae said, "I thought I might try and fashion a dress. I've been wearing the same few things since, well ... you know. But it's okay if you're saving it. I understand and, as I said, I didn't mean to pry into your things."

Jeb smiled too. "I think that would be a lovely idea. Anything you find here you can use, you use it. Anything you need, you just let me know."

Shae looked down and Jeb could see the color come into her own cheeks. "You're a good man, Jeb," she said. "And you're going to be late to work."

He grinned. "It's all right. I know the boss."

The woman's giggle in his ears, Jeb walked out to start the new day.

Chapter Twelve

A few days later, as they all sat eating dinner the evening before the fair, Jeb felt that all his time spent thinking, pondering, looking for problems and considering his options, had finally come to a head. He'd known plenty of men, and women as well for that matter, who were expert liars. He'd seen men bluff at cards, cheat at dice, and spin a yarn even the best jury would fall for. But no matter how many flim-flammers and confident men he'd come across in his days, there was always one person a fella couldn't lie to. At least not very effectively. And that was the man himself.

Since the morning with Ben, the episode had played itself over and over in his mind. It wasn't that there was anything particularly special about it. Toys break; toys get fixed. He helped people. That was his job. But something about that particular incident, some undercurrent of normalcy in it, made it exceptional almost due to its ordinariness. As Jeb had run through the details again and again, seeing Shae's smile, the way the boy interacted with him, what he kept thinking more than anything was, it felt normal. The sheer normalcy of helping the child, of smiling at the woman, of saying his goodbyes before heading out to a day at the office, it was something he hadn't felt in so long.

Perhaps it was something he'd never taken the time to realize he missed. He'd been so lost in his loss, in the absence of his wife, in the absence of his own children, that he'd never really been able to see that his life was still moving forward. Now, after that one small incident, the signs were everywhere.

Jeb had tried to look at it scientifically. He'd tried to poke holes in his idea, see how others would see it, figure out where it was he was making a false step. But in the end, at least in his own counsel, he couldn't find a problem. Granted, the choice wasn't entirely up to him. But then again, as he'd grown older, he'd become a man to balance his thoughts and his actions more fairly. Each had a place, but lingering too long with one or the other never accomplished anything worth doing.

So, in the midst of dinner, without any other idea in mind, he'd sat down his fork, looked at the children, and then finally turned to the woman across from him.

"Shae," he started, trying to formulate the precise words he'd practiced in the office all day but finding himself tongue-tied in the moment. The woman looked at him, waiting.

"You see," he started again. "It seems to me that we find ourselves in a situation that, well, it's not something either one of us ever could've, or would've, planned on. But at the same time, from where I sit at least, it feels like we've come into something that, well ..." He trailed off, wanting to start over. He looked down at his plate, up at the woman again. If he wasn't mistaken, the slightest trace of a smile was playing at the corners of her mouth.

"It's like this," he said. "Out here, well, it don't do for a good woman like yourself to be stuck on her own like this. You got the kids to think of. And yourself as well. And it ain't right for you to spend your days working for ..." No, this wasn't going as he wanted at all.

"The thing is," he tried again. "Maybe you've been hearing things about ... well, no. See, convenient ain't really the word I'm wanting here ..."

"Jeb," the woman said, beaming at him, finally saving him from himself. "I assume there can only be two things you might be getting at here. One of them, I suppose, would be that you're about to ask me to leave. Or ..." She held up a finger as he started to say something. "Or, you have something else in mind. And it would be unfair of me to not say I've been thinking about the same thing."

"So, you … would?" he asked.

Shae laughed. "Oh I might, but I'm not going to settle for that type of question. I want to hear the words, Jebediah."

The man felt himself flush in spite of her calming expression.

"Shae," he said, reaching across the table to take her hand, "it would make me a very proud man if you would do me the honor of being my wife."

Daisy babbled obliviously on, but even Ben seemed to perk up at the words, even if he didn't fully grasp what was being said.

"The honor would be mine," Shae said and Jeb could see just the hint of tears rimming her eyes.

***

The wedding took place the next day at the fair. Shae, perhaps belying a bit of her foresight, had fashioned herself a beautiful dress from the fabric she'd mentioned to Jeb not even a week previously. Word had spread quickly through the town, despite the short notice, and the celebration had been lively and thorough. Shae had come with flowers in her hair; Jeb in his freshly-pressed uniform and newly-shined boots. Ben, while originally dressed to the nines, had quickly fallen prey to the excitement of not just the wedding, but the fair and the sense of celebration that permeated the air around them.

The night had been filled with dancing, toasts to the new bride, pats on the back and handshakes for the groom, and not a small amount of gifts from the town's well-wishers. As a small band had played on in the background, Jeb had held his new wife on the makeshift dance floor, spinning her, moving her close, and once, in spite of his own bashfulness, kissed her boldly and proudly to the cheers of those around them.

As the night grew late, Jeb spotted Ben fast asleep in a wooden folding chair off to one side of the large tent brought in for the fair. An armful of treasures were clutched to his chest, both those given to the boy and those he "won" from generous men running the games that evening. Daisy had been taken home by Grace hours beforehand. Jeb led Shae over to a pair of empty chairs by Ben.

"I think we finally wore him out," Jeb said, looking down at the boy.

"I think we wore me out as well," Shae laughed, placing her on his.

"Time to go home?" Jeb asked, surprised at the smile the words brought to the woman's face.

"Home," she repeated. "That's a word I wasn't sure I'd ever use again." She paused, looking into his eyes. "It sounds lovely, Jeb. I can't ever thank you enough for giving me, us, a home again."

He smiled at her. "I could say the same to you, Shae. Before you all come along, I was just a feller with a house."

***

About an hour later, the new couple sat on the front porch of their home. Ben had been safely tucked away, waking only long enough to pull his new toys closer to him as Jeb and Shae had tucked him into bed. As the wind blew through the cool night, the pair sat next to one another in their rocking chairs, enjoying the peaceful silence after what had been a rambunctious evening.

"It feels different," Shae said, breaking the quiet. "I know that sounds silly, but being here, now, with you. I'm the sheriff's wife," she giggled to herself, reaching over to take his hand.

Jeb smiled. "Yeah, you're stuck with me now, I'd say."

Shae swatted at his arm. "Well, there's no place I'd rather be."

Just then, the clatter of hooves came pounding out of the darkness. A horse and rider rushed up to the house, Jeb noting at the last moment it was his deputy, Aaron, leaping from the saddle as the horse skidded to a halt.

"Jeb," he cried, breathless. "You gotta come quick! They burned it down!"

Jeb was on his feet immediately, his hand unconsciously reaching down for where his revolver should've hung. Shae, he noticed, had leapt up as well.

"What is it, Aaron?"

"The sheriff's station," Aaron said, leaning on the porch rail to catch his breath. "They burned it to the ground. And they're gone. All of 'em."

Just then Shae reappeared, Jeb's gunbelt held out in her hands. He glanced over at her.

"Go," she said.

Jeb snatched the belt and raced down the front steps to go fetch his horse. "I'll be back," he called out to her.

"I know," she said softly, almost to herself.

Chapter Thirteen

In the early morning hours, as Jeb and Aaron kicked through the charred wreckage that had so recently been their base of operations, across town, Edward had gathered his newly reformed crew for a meeting. More than half of them still reeked of the smoke from the fire, and bickering was incessant about how everything had gone down.

Finally, Edward rapped on the wooden table in front of him with his knuckles. "I think that covers everything with regard to that particular operation," he said.

"But sir," one of the men started. "You warn't there. I'm tellin' ya, if I hadn't got outta there when I did, I wouldn't be sittin' here now. I 'preciate them springin' us and all, but hot damn, they coulda waited till we was outside afore lightin' the place up like that."

"Yes, well," Edward said, grinning slightly. "You are here now, so we can consider it a success. If you prefer, think of it as an impromptu test of your quick thinking."

The man looked as if he were about to retort, but caught Edward's eye and kept silent.

"Whether you all are chums or not is frankly none of my concern," Vanderheist began. "What is my concern is that you all work properly, smoothly, and successfully as a unit. I have my hands more than full, as some of you may know, and the only reason you are here," he paused to look around the room, "the only reason, is to ensure that things continue moving forward.

"Some of you had the unfortunate experience of being arrested. As you can see, in my crew, we take care of our own. You needn't worry about sitting and rotting in a jail cell somewhere just because some sheriff has a stroke of luck and a tracker on his side."

There was a murmur of approval from the men in the room with him.

"I am in the business of making money," Vanderheist continued. "When I make money, you make money. When I don't, you don't. It's all very simple. However, and I trust I won't be stretching the bounds of your intellect when I make this logical jump, but I feel it must be said, the very fact of the situation is, when I have problems, you have problems. We cannot work individually and expect any amount of success to come of it. If that were the case, none of you would be here right now."

A few of the men started to chuckle, but the icy look in Edward's eyes quickly silenced them. The man was deadly serious.

"It's come to my attention that the two of you who were lucky enough to not immediately be shot by Mr. Barnett and his deputy were in a unique position. My understanding from those in the know is that, should either of you have given the sheriff enough information, he was willing to let you walk free. Given that all of you were still safely tucked away in your cells, I must assume his particular level was not met."

"That's right," one of the men said. "He kept thinkin' he'd break one of us, but we knowed you'd come for us."

Vanderheist looked at the man, his gaze lingering for a moment before moving slowly across the face of the other recently incarcerated man.

"Nevertheless," Edward said, "Trevor informs me that while you did not give Mr. Barnett enough information to free yourselves, there was some exchange of information. Now would be the time for us to discuss that."

The two men looked at one another. "Smitty," one growled, "what'd you do?"

"Me?" the man jumped up. "What'd you do? I didn't tell 'em nothin'!"

"Well, someone did," Vanderheist interrupted. "That, or Trevor has been making up tales. I do feel I must add, though, Mr. Clark, your reputation didn't come out of this spotless, either."

"Now, look," the first man said, whipping his attention away from Smitty and turning it to his boss. "You know how it is. You gotta tell these fellers somethin'. I don't know what this one here did," he hitched a thumb over at his companion, "but I didn't give 'em nothin' they could use against you, or any of us. Hell, I don't even remember half of what I said, on account of I was just makin' it up."

"Ah," Vanderheist said. "So your argument is that you only told them lies. Or is your argument that you only told them useless truths?"

"Well, see," the man started, but Vanderheist held up a hand, cutting him off.

"As I mentioned earlier, when I have a problem, we all have a problem. Do you agree with that, Mr. Clark?" he looked over to the other man. "Mr. Smith?"

The two outlaws nodded, silently.

"Now for us to move forward in this enterprise, we need to solve these problems. As I said, we work as a unit here. Thankfully, Trevor has come up with a solution that I think is both elegant and simple. If the two of you could join him for a moment, he will explain."

Warily, the two men stood up and followed Trevor out the side door of the small meeting house. A silence weighed the air in the room as the remainder of Vanderheist's men, those involved in the jailbreak and those brought in for the evening sat quietly, most avoiding eye contact with the leader.

Vanderheist crossed one leg over the other, plucking at the crisp crease on the knee of his trousers.

A few seconds later, a gunshot rang out. There was a cry, the sound of a brief scuffle, another shot, and then silence again. A moment later, Trevor stepped back into the room, reloading the empty chambers of his revolver. He nodded at Vanderheist and then took his place standing by the wall.

"I'm sure you will agree," Vanderheist said, "simple, elegant, and now, for those of us still breathing at least, we can move forward." He leaned forward on the table, folding his hands and looking at the men individually as he spoke.

"The first order of business, or," he paused, smiling slightly to himself, "after you make those bodies disappear, of course, the first order of business is to find replacements. I'm sure most of you are already hoping I don't recall who brought Mr. Clark and Mr. Smith into our ranks. The fact is, I do."

After a second, Trevor stepped forward. "It was me, sir."

"Indeed it was," Vanderheist said. "I'd like you all to remember that. Perhaps a mistake will happen now and again. Trevor reported his mistake to me. Not only that, he presented a solution to this problem." Vanderheist looked around the room. "That, and only that, is the reason Trevor here is still breathing.

"I don't have time for games. I will not tolerate mediocrity. Get rid of the bodies. Find me new men. I expect a full crew in here this evening. We already have saloon owners waiting on liquor. And don't get me started on the guns. Now move!"

As the men hurried to the exit, Vanderheist gestured Trevor over to the table. "Excellent work, Trevor," he said.

"Thank you, sir."

"You're proving yourself useful. Therefore, I have a new task for you."

"Yes, sir."

"I need you to figure out what we can do with this sheriff. And don't tell me 'shoot him.' Obviously, we can do that. But I'd like to do so with a little less showmanship than took place at the jail this evening. Follow the man around, learn his schedule. Find the weaknesses. When the moment comes, I want us ready to pounce."

"Yes, sir," Trevor said.

Vanderheist watched as the man rushed out the door after his companions. *A well-oiled machine,* Edward thought. *Or at least, close enough for now.*

Chapter Fourteen

The next morning, Jeb and Aaron sat at a table in a small eatery in the middle of town, two cups of coffee between them. The day was steamy, cloudless. They'd met at the remains of the sheriff's station, not out of any particular plan, but both simply showing up at the place out of ingrained habit. With few words shared between them, Jeb had walked off toward the diner.

"I know what you're thinking," Aaron finally said. "And I wish I could help, but we were already pushing it the first time I took you out there. We go too far with this and we lose one of the few helps we got in this town."

Jeb looked at him. "We don't go out there, it ain't much help anyway."

"I know," Aaron said. "And look, I understand."

"Do you?" Jeb barked.

Aaron sat back in his chair, startled by the outburst but not completely losing his calm demeanor. "I understand as best as I can."

Jeb sighed. "I know it. It's just a lot. And I don't mean for me. I mean Shae, the kids. Maybe Daisy don't know much, but Ben's old enough to see something ain't right. This amount of jumping around, sure, it might be an adventure at first, but we gotta get them someplace safe, and we gotta do it fast. Every one of them boys we had in lock-up would be more than happy to put a bullet in me and you both. You ain't got a lot of people around, but after what they done before, I ain't leaving Shae to any more run-ins with that gang."

"I know it, Jeb. I was there with you from the start of all this. Alls I'm saying is, we gotta come up with a new plan. Just traipsing up and meeting with the tribe ain't how they do it. Now, they stood for it last time, but you don't know 'em like I do. Besides me, you're the only white man I've ever seen sit down and palaver with the chief like that. It ain't something you just decide to do and go do it. They got their own rules out there."

"Aaron," Jeb said, "unless you got a better idea, that's exactly what I've decided to do."

Aaron slapped the table. "For what, Jeb? What're you gonna accomplish except burn a bridge? You trust me, don't ya?"

Jeb nodded slowly.

"Then trust me now," Aaron said. "No good can come of you showing up there without a welcome. Them people have been trying to stay away from us for a long time and now you wanna go chase 'em down again. Why you think they stay away? Cause folks like us don't leave 'em alone when they ask."

Jeb turned his coffee mug on the wooden table, looking at the black liquid. "I know you're right. I really do. But I'm asking you to trust me as well. Don't you reckon if I had any other idea we'd be working on it already? If I had some hiding place, Shae and the kids wouldn't already be there? Only reason I'm not at the house right now is so I'm an easy target. The more eyes on me, the less on them."

Aaron ran his hands through his hair. "I know it, I know it. I just figure..." He trailed off, an unsure look on his face. "Look, I hate to bring it up, but ain't you got some people in Dallas?"

Jeb sniffed. "What good would it do me if I did? No secret I spent time there. You and everybody else in town know that. Shae turns up missing, where you think is the first place they'd look? Besides, having people and having people I'd put her with is two different things."

Aaron sat for a minute. "So that it," he said finally.

"That's it," Jeb said. "If it's this hard for me and you to get out there with them Comanche, there ain't a safer place on earth for Shae and the kids."

"You're right on that account," Aaron said. "But I don't know how you're gonna do it."

Jeb shrugged, drank the rest of his coffee, and stood up. "All I'm asking from you is to ride out with me. The rest of it ain't your concern."

"And if it doesn't work?"

Jeb looked out the window at the dusty street. "Ain't got much choice," he said.

***

The following day, Jeb sat in the same shaded area on the outskirts of the tribe. A plethora of animals was being led back among the native people, some laden with blankets, tools, anything Jeb could buy, part with, or otherwise lay his hands on. Across from him, the chief sat, stoic.

As an ox slowly lumbered past, led by one of the tribesmen, the chief looked at Jeb. "Gifts from your people often come at a high price."

Jeb, his hands folded and hanging between his knees, looked up at the man. "Ain't much of a gift then, is it?" He pushed his hat back on his head. "And as far as my people go, I ain't here representing them. I'm coming to you as just me, one man."

"As have many before you. Why should I think this will be any different? I granted Aaron's request once, partially on the condition that it not happen again, and yet ..." He spread his hands in front of him. "Here we sit. Again."

Jeb thought for a moment. "When I come before, I didn't have no intention of coming back myself," he finally said. "I respect your wishes. I keep myself and my people to ourselves, much as I can, leastwise. If I had another way of handling this, you best bet I would. I appreciate that you and your people want to be left alone. Well, despite what it might look like, I do, too. In fact, I ain't much one to ask for help, neither. But I'm not a fool. I ain't here to cause problems, but I know when I've got a problem that's bigger than me. Way I see it, you may have the same problem."

The chief looked at the sheriff, weighing his words. "Perhaps starting with bribery was not the wisest choice."

Jeb shook his head slowly, trying to keep his patience. "I get it," he said. "And you want me to run these animals back into town, I'll do it. But don't get turned around on why I brought 'em here. I'm askin' for your help and I pay for that."

"Extravagantly."

Jeb looked into the chief's eyes. "We ain't talking about mending a fence," he said. "This is my wife, our kids. And every moment they're in that town, they're in danger."

"So you direct the danger to us?" the chief asked. "Your deal is sounding worse and worse."

Jeb laughed. He meant no disrespect, but the response was so unexpected. "Way I see it, ain't no safer place in the world they could be."

The slightest hint of a smile passed across the chief's lips. "You speak the truth," he said. "And perhaps, if I can trust what I've heard from Aaron, what I've seen of you, perhaps we are fighting a common enemy."

Jeb leaned forward. "What've you heard?"

"This foreigner," the chief started, "he is relentless in his harassment of my people. Those who acquiesce are sent to join him. We have no place for that type of man here. But still, he comes back. His guns, his alcohol, everywhere we turn he is pressuring us more and more. Other tribes have given in. We shall not."

"Then help us get rid of him."

For the first time, the chief smiled. "You think we need your help?"

Jeb grinned back, albeit grimly. "I suppose I do owe you a thanks for not letting things get too bloody out here."

"We want violence no more than you do."

"But sometimes it comes to that," Jeb said.

The chief nodded.

Jeb looked over at Aaron. "I think we might be able to avoid that this time. You still expect them fellas back around the first of the month?"

The chief nodded again.

"All right," Jeb said. "You take care of Shae and the kids, I'll deal with Vanderheist." He stood, extending a hand. After a long pause, the chief stood, grasping Jeb's hand in his own.

Chapter Fifteen

In Amarillo, Vanderheist sat in the bunkhouse with a small group of his best men. Trevor, having spent a few hot, dusty days hiding out in the shadows around the sheriff's ranch had finally returned with as much information as he was able to muster. Vanderheist often wondered how much he could trust his men. It was part of the lifestyle, he supposed. When one laid down with dogs, one got up with fleas. Or so he'd been told.

But, he thought, that all depended on how one treated the dogs. And he'd ensured that his dogs were very, very well taken care of. Amarillo hadn't been the smoothest of operations so far. He supposed this was partially due to complacency on his own part. Working west had been filled with ups and down, but coming down through Oklahoma had been amazingly easy. Other than a few dust-ups out around Omaha, Vanderheist had been on a streak of favorable luck, so he supposed, in some ways perhaps, he was due for a bit of an uphill battle.

Besides, it kept him sharp. And these men, though perhaps not the sharpest themselves, had a few things going for them. One was greed, though that was hardly difficult to find out in the more uncivilized parts of the country. The gall to act on that greed was another crucial aspect that Vanderheist hadn't struggled to track down. Every man had a price; Edward just happened to be in a position to pay that price, regardless of how high it sounded. And that, of course, was where the mental capacity of his soldiers came into play. A smart manwaisn't easily dazzled by the bag of coins or stack of banknotes Vanderheist would offer initially. A smart man would hold out, ask questions, perhaps take the time to consider that a man in Vanderheist's position certainly didn't get there by "making ends meet."

But that was precisely where the men in the bunkhouse lived, at the stage in life where a big payday was the dream, and a missed one meant a hungry night. And besides, it also made the men highly expendable. That, if nothing else, was the one thing these so-called gunslingers *were* smart enough to grasp. Vanderheist merely needed to dangle the right carrot, as they said. He could be kind, or he could be cruel. The choice meant little to him, so long as his goals were accomplished. If it came from a bag of money or a bullet, it really meant little to him.

And what he truly enjoyed about men like Trevor was that Trevor had seen both sides of Vanderheist numerous times, yet still had the good sense to know it meant nothing whatsoever.

So, when Trevor claimed to have gathered what Vanderheist needed to know, the man felt reasonably certain the man had been careful enough to not come back with less than what was requested.

If so, well, Trevor could simply become another object lesson for the other men standing in the lamp light with them.

"Since they come back, they been at it like clockwork," Trevor was saying. "Early mornings, late nights, but it's every day. Them two boys is runnin' theyselves ragged, so we hit 'em in the middle of the night, they ain't got a prayer. 'Specially we give 'em a few more days of it. Run out and hit them Indians, give 'em something to keep busy with, 'specially something needing a long ride like that, we won't even have to worry about 'em wakin' up before we plug 'em."

Vanderheist sat in front of the group, one leg crossed over the other, his hands folded on his knee.

"Not bad, Trevor," he said. "Not bad at all. I have to admit, you've given me even more than I expected."

"Welcome, sir," Trevor said, stepping back somewhat, seeming to not enjoy too much of Vanderheist's direct attention.

"I would pose a question to you, though," Edward said, watching Trevor pale and enjoying the moment perhaps a little too much. "If we're going to run these boys ragged before we shoot them, why stop with the tribe? Why not burn down a church or rob the bank? Why not become horse thieves? Why not ride through town, guns blazing, every single day?"

Trevor stood quietly, unsure if he was supposed to answer. Finally, as Vanderheist's gaze bored into him, he ventured a few words. "Well, sir, I … uh, well, I reckon that could work."

Vanderheist smiled. "Very noncommittal of you, Trevor. However, I'll spare you the trouble. The reason is, there is no reason. Why let the sheriff and his man wander about any longer than we need to? True, as you've stated, they will be worn down. But they are already. True, we will have the element of surprise on our side. But we do already. And I wonder, Trevor, I wonder if by going after the chief first, if we might lose some of that surprise."

"Yes, sir," Trevor said.

"Yes, what?"

"Yes, you're right, sir, I reckon."

Vanderheist leaned on the table in front of him. "I hired you boys for very specific reasons. One is that you know the area. Another is that you're not afraid to get your hands dirty. What I did not hire you for, however, was your ability to come up with a plan. So" — he looked from Trevor to the men around the room — "you may all rest easy on that front. Now, while I do appreciate Trevor's input, I'd like to present to you my version of events."

He paused, looking around at the men, ostensibly waiting for their full attention, but mostly just enjoying the discomfort his silence could cause. Whatever he needed from these men, more than anything, he needed their fear of him. A healthy, respectful fear.

"This is what I propose. First off, with regard to our native friends, unless I sorely miss the mark, they want no more to do with us than we do with them. Their support for our cause has been less than enthusiastic and, while everyone is entitled to his opinion, I cannot stand for the outright disregard this particular chief has been giving to our operation.

"Problems arise and problems must be dealt with. Swiftly, more often than not. But we are in a particular circumstance where our problems are lining up. Word may spread that one tribe has stood up against us, scoffed at our more than generous offers. I say, all right. Let the word spread. Let it get to every ear within riding distance. Because after we deal with the sheriff, we will deal with the Comanche, and then word can spread about the repercussions of balking at our business deals."

A few of the men voiced agreement, some simply sounding excited at the idea of bloodshed.

"Our first concern," Vanderheist continued, "is the law here. Perhaps if we had more time, we could come up with something a bit more elegant, but I'm not one to dilly-dally, as the saying goes." A few snickers came from the men at the use of the somewhat childish phrase. Vanderheist paused, glaring at the men until silence returned. "I'm also not one who likes being considered a joke, as some of you would do well to keep in mind." His hand rested almost nonchalantly on the barrel of the revolver strapped to his hip under his suit jacket.

"As I was saying, if we attack the tribe first, as Trevor here suggested, we only alert the sheriff that we're making moves. Perhaps the tribe will react if we attack the sheriff first. But something tells me they prefer to leave us to solve our own problems. So, with that in mind, I'm sending some of you off with Trevor this evening. Your job is to do as he says. In this instance, consider his instructions my instructions. Once we've got Mr. Barnett taken care of, we will move on to deal with the next item on our list. Have I made myself clear?"

General murmurs from the crowd met his question. Vanderheist looked to Trevor. "I do hope the information you gathered will be sufficient," the boss said. "You're about to stake your life on it."

"I won't let you down sir," Trevor said, turning to the men.

Chapter Sixteen

The following evening, Jeb sat in the office above the mercantile shop he'd been using as a makeshift office for the last two days. He had his feet up on the windowsill, looking out down the main street of Amarillo. The people wandered back and forth, running their late errands, leading tired horses back to the stables for the evening. A lone wagon made its way up to the shop below him, the slow pace belying a full day of deliveries coming to a close.

It was a good town, Jeb thought. Sure, that wasn't what had brought him to Amarillo originally, but it was what had kept him around. Different cities had different feelings, or at least that's how he'd always experienced it. Some were exciting, some were sleepy. Some were dangerous or risky. Some chewed folks up and spat them out like an old plug of tobacco. But Amarillo had always felt different, unique somehow. Perhaps it was the balance. The town had its moments of excitement, but never uproar. It had its hard times as well, but never something hopeless. Perhaps it was just Jeb himself, maturing along with the town in some ways. The two had certainly seen a lot of one another over the years.

Jeb thought back to his younger days, before the move to Dallas, back when he and Aaron had just been two little troublemakers running up and down the streets and alleyways, raising hell out in the pastures or wandering off through the woods outside of town. Amarillo was as much a part of Jeb as anything else, he was realizing. Folks say nothing lasts forever, but Jeb knew the city had been there long before he came around and would likely be there long after he departed this world.

Or, at least, he was going to do his best to ensure that was the case. Not for himself, maybe not even for the folks he could see passing by below him, though they were a part of it. In his heart, if he really let himself be true, it was for Shae. It was for Ben and Daisy, the ones who would inherit whatever town he left them. It could be a place of happiness, opportunity. Or it could be somewhere they'd run from at the first chance. Jeb knew the odds were slowly stacking up against him, but he'd never been one to shy away from a long shot.

Besides, if the town needed someone to stand up for it, someone to jolt it awake and show that there was something here worth fighting for, why, he reckoned he was just as good as the next fellow to take that stand.

Plus, he had the badge to do so.

"Jeb?"

Though the sound startled him, the only noticeable movement was of his hand to the butt of his gun. Jeb's eyes adjusted quickly, the focus leaving the people in the street below and honing in on the reflection in the glass in front of him.

"Easy," he heard Aaron say. "Just me."

Jeb watched Aaron's image pull a chair across the room and set it in front of the desk. The sheriff swiveled around in his chair as Aaron sighed, pulled off a dusty hat, and stretched his legs out, propping his boots on the corner of the desk.

"Long day?" Jeb asked.

Aaron laughed a little, smiling. "I was about to ask you the same thing. I said your name three times before you turned around."

Jeb cocked his head to the side.

"Ah," Aaron waved his hand in the air. "You ain't gettin' rusty. My ma used to say I could sneak up on a ghost. Ain't something I was tryin' to do. Just habit these days."

Jeb smiled. "How old was you the first time you went out there to that tribe? Eight? Ten?"

Aaron looked up at the ceiling. "Yeah, about that, I'd say. Certainly no more."

"Lifetime ago, ain't it?"

Aaron smiled. "Seems that way sometimes, I reckon. We really crammed a lotta life into these years though."

Jeb laughed. "I ain't gonna argue with you there, friend."

Aaron rubbed at his eyes with one hand. "I ain't complainin' about none of it, of course, but I tell ya, Jeb, any time you wanna take a breather, you just let me know."

"Yeah," the sheriff said. "Wish it was that easy."

"Wish in one hand, as they say," Aaron smiled. "What's the real plan though, boss? You come up with anything?"

Jeb leaned his forearms on the desk, looking down at his interlaced fingers. "I do. And I hate to tell ya, it's gonna be another long day of riding for us."

Aaron nodded. "Ah, well, I kinda figured on that sooner or later. Shae and them?"

"Yeah," Jeb said. "Now that we got the okay with the chief, ain't no sense in waiting any longer."

"What'd she say about it?"

Jeb smiled just a little. "I'll tell her tonight. Didn't see no reason getting her worried."

"Probably for the best," Aaron said. "Less people know what you're thinking, safer everybody is."

"My thoughts as well."

"I guess that answers my question then," Aaron said.

"What was that?"

"What the plan was for tomorrow. I know we've been trying to keep on everybody at once lately, but it can't go on forever. I figured you were getting as antsy as I am to do something besides watch folks."

Jeb nodded. "And as soon as we get Shae and the kids out of town, we'll get to actin' on that."

"Nothing'd make me happier," Aaron said.

"I'm glad to hear that," Jeb said. "I ain't real keen on the two of us leaving the town again, but I also ain't real sure that chief's gonna wanna see me again any time soon, even if we are working towards the same end."

"You want me to run Shae out there on my own?"

Jeb thought for a moment. "To be honest with ya, Aaron, I don't know what I want." He paused. "I take that back. What I want is to not be running my family all over the countryside. What I want is to not be worrying if I should be home right now instead of sitting here talking to you. What I want is things to settle back to the way they was."

"The way they was when?" Aaron asked.

Jeb thought for a moment, then let out a quiet laugh. "You got a point. How about, the way they was before Vanderheist came callin'?"

"I'd settle for that."

"Well," Jeb said, standing up. "We'll get there. First thing we gotta do is run them out to the Comanche. We get that taken care of tomorrow, then we get to solving this next problem."

"Sounds good," Aaron said. "Need me to come help you out at the house?"

"Nah," Jeb said, taking his hat from a peg on the wall. "We ain't packin' to move, just to make a visit. Least, I hope so."

Aaron nodded. "It will be." The deputy stood up, looking down at his hat for a moment before putting it on his head. "This time tomorrow, things're gonna look a whole lot different," he said.

"You got that right," Jeb said. "And I don't think old Vanderheist is gonna like the view."

Chapter Seventeen

That night, Shae sat in the dim light of one kerosene lantern, Ben tucked in his bed, looking over at her as she held Daisy to her chest, slowly rocking back and forth in a chair next to him.

"So, the donkey, the dog, and the cat kept walking until they came to a farm where there lived a rooster," Shae said quietly. "'Where are you headed?' asked the rooster."

"To be ..." Ben yawned, trying his best to stay awake for the story Shae had told him countless times. "City ... musicians ..." The boy's eyelids closed before the second word was out of his mouth.

"That's right," Shae said quietly. "'We're going to be city musicians,' the horse said. 'Why don't you come along and join us?'"

She paused, waiting for the boy to protest as he usually did when the story lagged for even a moment. Instead, she saw him simply sigh and snuggle farther down under the blankets, despite the warm evening air. Shae stood and walked over to the bassinet, laying Daisy down for what she hoped would be a full night's sleep. Not for the first time, she was amazed at how quickly the children had adapted to their new home. Ben, she knew, would have questions one day. He was old enough to. And he was a curious enough boy to have questions about nearly anything as it was.

Shae stood for a moment, watching Daisy sleep. Her little daughter had perhaps surprised her more than her son. Daisy had always been a light and finicky sleeper. But since they'd come to Jeb's, her usual half a dozen trips to soothe the crying child had been reduced to two, sometimes even just once per night. Jeb claimed the noise never bothered him, and she knew the long days he'd been putting in had likely helped this. The man slept like a log. Nevertheless, in some tiny, almost forgotten ways, Shae still found herself thinking like a guest, not like the woman of the house.

These were his children to help raise now. They, she, were his family.

Shae leaned down and kissed Daisy on the forehead, then walked quietly over to do the same for Ben. She brushed the boy's hair to the side. He had done well and despite his best efforts to hide it, she knew he hadn't always slept the night through either. But, the dark circles she'd grown accustomed to seeing had faded over the weeks in the sheriff's house. Perhaps, she thought, she wasn't the only one who somehow felt safe there.

The thought gave her only a moment's pause. Perhaps it was unkind of her to think such things, but kindness only got on so far. And whatever the reason, she couldn't deny she felt safer with Jeb than she ever had before.

She walked over and turned down the wick on the lantern, extinguishing the light in the room. Shae paused at the window, a curtain in either hand, as she saw Jeb's figure walking back from the small stable where he kept his horse. Another late night for the man. It wasn't unusual. To be honest, these kinds of days and nights were all she'd experienced since knowing Jeb as merely more than the sheriff, the boss of her late husband.

But she did find herself holding out hope that Jeb Barnett the man would come home one evening, that she would be able to spend a simple evening with her husband. They were wed now, after all, and yet things only seemed busier, more hectic than they had before. No sense in wasting what moments she was giving though, she thought, pulling the curtains closed and slipping out the door, leaving it just slightly ajar behind her as she made her way toward the stairs.

Halfway down, Jeb met her coming up.

"Evening," he said, smiling in spite of the lines of fatigue she could see on his face.

"You as well," she turned to walk back up the stairs with him.

"Kids bedded?" he asked.

"Just," she paused at the landing, allowing the man to pass by her on his way to the main bedroom.

It wasn't something they'd discussed, not something she'd felt right pressing, but often in the night, she'd moved back to her old sleeping area in the spare room. His sleep was fitful, filled with the tossings and turnings of dangerous dreams she didn't want to ask about just yet. In the mornings she'd always made sure to be downstairs, preparing breakfast for the family before he awoke. Perhaps her slight misdirection worked, though she often wondered if he awoke in the night, wondering where she was.

If so, she certainly couldn't keep up the charade for long. It didn't do right by him, and she certainly didn't want him interpreting it in the wrong way.

In the bedroom, Jeb sat down on the side of the bed, pulling his boots off, a tired sigh escaping his lips.

"These days are going to catch up with you," she said, sitting on the bed beside him.

"Yes," he said, hanging his hat on the bedpost, then turning to her. "But they ain't got me licked yet," he said, smiling. "'Sides, you're the one here with them two yahoos all day long. Some folks'd say I got the easy part of the deal."

She laughed, looking down at her hands. "It's not so bad," she said. "Other than Ben asking when you'll be home just as soon as you walk out the door."

Jeb laughed. "We gotta get that boy a pocket watch."

"And we've got to teach him how to read it as well."

"One step at a time."

She smiled, her hands twisting in one another. Jeb surprised her by reaching over and putting one of his calloused, dark hands on hers.

"What's really on your mind?" he asked.

"Oh, it's nothing," she shook her head, a few of her fingers lacing around his. "I just ..."

She trailed off, unsure how to express just what she was thinking. It wasn't that she didn't trust the man; nothing could be farther from the truth. But when he was gone...

"You worry?" Jeb said, finishing the sentences, both spoken and unspoken, for her.

Shae nodded, wanting to speak but already feeling a waver in her throat.

"C'mere," Jeb put an arm around her shoulders, pulling her close. "I rode out a lot of days in my life, and you know what always happened, no matter what? I come back."

Shae wiped at the corner of her eye with the back of her hand. "I know. I know. But ..."

Jeb took her by the shoulders and turned her toward him. "There's a lot of words that could come on the tail end of that 'but,' and I can tell ya now, I don't care too much what they are. Long as you and them kids is here, I got more reason than any man to make sure I come home at night. I know you probably heard that before, so I don't blame ya for wondering if I mean it. Fact is though, Missus Shae Barnett" — she felt herself flush at the use of her new name — "only reason I been out late is to make sure we both got us a safe place to come home to."

"I know," she sighed. "I'm just being silly in some ways."

"Hey now," Jeb rubbed at her cheek. "I don't spend my time with silly women, so you must be wrong there."

Shae smiled in spite of herself.

"We need to talk though," Jeb said. "And you ain't gonna like hearing it any more than I like saying it, but you're a strong woman, and strong women do what's best, don't they?"

She nodded. "When we have to," she tried to laugh a little.

"Well, this one'll be easy on you. Think of it as an adventure. Or, at least, that's how we're gonna sell it to Benny, so the more we're on the same side, the smoother this will go."

"You're sending us away, aren't you?"

"Not far. And not for long," Jeb said.

Shae sat quietly as he explained the plan he and his deputy had come up with. She couldn't argue with the man, no matter how much she wished she could. And it wasn't that he wouldn't listen. No, the frustrating part was that there was no argument to be made. He was right. Whatever was going to take place in Amarillo, she wanted her children far away from it.

"I'm worried, Jeb," she said after he'd finished his explanation, after she'd taken a long, thoughtful pause.

"Tell ya the truth, I ain't real keen on it either," he said, surprising her. "But fact is, I'm less keen on us worrying."

She smiled a little. "Us, huh? Surely the sheriff doesn't worry."

He grinned over at her. "Don't you go tellin' nobody. I got a reputation to keep."

"Your secret is safe with me," she said.

"Well," he cupped her cheek in his hand and looked into her eyes, "just to be extra safe, why don't you stay in here tonight?"

Shae wanted to protest, wanted to be shocked that he'd known all along, but before she could say anything, she felt his lips on hers, and let herself fall into his embrace.

Chapter Eighteen

When Jeb awoke, he at first thought it had merely been more dreams. The nights of the last few weeks had been hard and the fire at the sheriff's station had only made things worse. No matter what he did during his waking hours, in the night, his mind let loose his greatest fears. Before, the risks had been his only to take, the danger directed at him. Now, for the first time in years, he had so much more to lose.

He lay in the dark, listening. Shae rustled the bedding slightly as she turned her head up to look at him from where she'd be laying on his chest.

"What is it?" she said.

"Nothing, honey," he said softly. "Probably just dreams."

"No," she sat up farther in the bed. "Do you smell that? I smell smoke."

Jeb furrowed his brows, getting out of bed and moving to the window. The bedroom was at the front of the house, so from his view, there was nothing but the empty nighttime street. He opened the pane and stuck his head out.

After a moment, he pulled himself back in, grabbing his shirt from the chair by the bed.

"What is it?" Shae asked, reaching to the floor for her dress.

"Don't know," Jeb said, buckling his gunbelt around his waist. "You stay inside."

"I'm going to check on the children," she said, an edge in her voice.

Jeb pulled his boots on, nodded to the woman, and headed for the stairs. At the top, he paused. "You hear anything, you hunker down. You're safe in here."

She looked at him and he could see the fear in her eyes. There was something else as well. Not doubt. He knew, somehow, after all she'd been through, she still had the ability to trust, to hope. But there was an uncertainty underneath it all. "I'll come back," he said.

She rushed over to him, squeezed his hand on the banister, and then hurried down the hall to slip into the kids' sleeping area.

Outside, Jeb moved cautiously, yet boldly. The window upstairs had given him a generally wide view of the front. But it didn't show him what was most important. He couldn't see down past the roof over the porch, couldn't tell who might be lurking on either side of the front door. Things that happened in the night, more specifically the men who made them happen, were often counting on someone to be uncertain, maybe foggy from sleep, maybe moving slower than usual. Jeb's years on his own had broken him of the habit.

Having checked the front of the house, he began to work his way around one side. There was a definite smell of smoke, the low crackle of a slow-burning flame. A few chickens pecked and strutted through the yard ahead of him, hunting through the dirt and grass for a late snack. After his gift to the Comanche, the chickens were nearly the only animals left on the ranch.

Jeb hesitated at the corner of the house, crouching down by the rain barrel, listening. He watched the birds wander back and forth in front of him. Chickens were the next best thing to a dog when it came to standing guard, or at least that's what his pa had always told him. The typically skittish birds would pause, cock a head to the side, but not once did they show him any sign of alarm that would come from another person too close by.

Moving fast and low, Jeb rounded the corner of the building, his gun already in his hand.

Darkness. Stillness.

Except for the barn, at least. Smoke was drifting out of the haymow. He couldn't see any flames yet. Probably a smoldering fire, the type that might even put itself out momentarily. Jeb continued on into the backyard, checking the shadows, listening for voices. At the barn door, he rolled it back on its rusty wheels, entering gun first. But, other than a few crackles and snaps from above him, the place was silent.

And then it dawned on him. If someone had wanted to burn the place down, sure, the haymow would likely have the most fuel for the fire, but it made more sense to start the fire on the first floor, in the corners ideally, letting the flames burn up into the structure as they naturally wanted to, not start it at the top and hope it burned down.

This had been merely to get him out of the house. And like a fool, he'd fallen for it.

Jeb raced back out of the barn, crossing the backyard without caution. Just as he came to the corner of the porch he felt himself tangled in a mess of arms, men grasping him from either side, pushing him back away from the door, away from his family.

Jeb fought at the men, twisting, kicking, trying helplessly to gain some kind of upper hand. Instead, a third man walked past, grinned with an icy politeness, and headed inside Jeb's house.

His revolver, dropped in the initial scuffle, had been kicked off somewhere into the darkness. Try as he might, Jeb couldn't get an arm free enough to reach one of the men's gunbelts. The worst part was the helplessness. He'd been outnumbered before, but he was usually the one getting the drop on the other party. Now, as the men expertly hooked their legs around his, pulling his arms behind him, Jeb had to fight even to keep his balance, much less position himself to any kind of advantage.

From in the house, Shae's voice suddenly cut through the darkness. Jeb can't make out the words, wishes he didn't have to hear them at all, because no matter what the woman was saying, he knew it was the sound of him letting her down. It was her greatest fear come to life that echoed through the stillness. Ben's voice, confused, then frightened, then crying. Daisy's fussy tears immediately joined to create a sad, heart-wrenching harmony. The quick, clear sound of a slap.

Jeb struggled more, rage filling his heart. He didn't care what he had to do, who he had to hurt. He needed to get to his wife. If it meant killing the men on either side of them, murdering them would come without a second thought. He didn't know their names — didn't need to. They were between him and his family.

Jeb jerked at his arms, tried to kick his legs, but the only response was laughter from the men, which simply infuriated him more. He could feel his shoulder straining at the socket, his knees twisting in unnatural ways, and through the pain, one thought came through. If he hurt himself, he'd be of no use to Shae. The fire in his heart burned no less brightly, but Jeb willed himself to calm his body. He had to stay focused. Everything he could learn in these next few moments could make the difference between life and death. Not necessarily for him. At this moment he'd gladly take a bullet for the woman and children inside. But with him out of the way, whatever plan these men had would likely become moot.

No, if they'd wanted him dead, he'd be dead already. This smelled of something else entirely. Jeb tried to relax his muscles, regain some semblance of balance. From inside the house, he realized, the sounds had settled as well. Now he could hear Shae talking quietly, no doubt trying to calm the children as they made their way back down the steps. Jeb braced himself for what he was about to see.

As the clean-cut gentleman ushered his family out, it took all of Jeb's self-control to appear calm, to make eye contact with Shae, willing her to understand things were going to be all right.

From somewhere inside, two other men followed the party to the front porch. Their leader whispered something to them and they took up positions on either side of Shae, who held Daisy in her arms, and Ben, who clung to his mother's leg, sniffling, his face buried in her calico dress.

Jeb's senses felt heightened in every way. He could feel the cool wind on the back of his neck. The chickens were silent, necks likely broken. So much for his theory there. He could feel the pulse in his biceps where the arms of his captors were clamped down on his. He smelled sweat, but not fear. Ahead of him, the deep blue of Shae's dress made the yellow cornflower pattern stand out even more. And approaching him across the yard, looking almost like an apparition in his clean gray suit, could only be one man.

"Vanderheist," Jeb said.

"I had hoped we'd meet under more pleasant conditions," the man said. Then giving Jeb a slight, cocky grin, corrected himself. "That's not entirely true, actually. I was hoping we'd never have to meet at all, but …" He shrugged. "Business is unpredictable at times."

"What kinda business we got that requires you to slip in here like a snake and threaten women and children?"

Vanderheist stopped just a few feet away from Jeb. It was as if the man had judged the distance precisely. Even if Jeb could free an arm, Vanderheist would still be just out of reach.

"The bravado of the west," Vanderheist said. "I'd heard so much about it when I was back on the East Coast and I must say, you certainly haven't let me down. Every mile I traveled in this direction, the threats and the egos became bigger. I must say, in a way, I think I would've been disappointed to have found anything else. Nevertheless, it comes with a price, and I believe you're seeing that now. Once again, if I'm not mistaken."

Jeb clenched his jaw, not wanting to take the bait, but needing to know his enemy.

"Sounds like you looked into me," Jeb said through gritted teeth. "What about you? I got a name. I got rumors. But other than that fancy suit, I can't say I know much about you. Why don't you call off your dogs and me and you can get to know one another man to man?"

Vanderheist grinned. "Please don't allow my appearance to give you the wrong impression, Mr. Barnett. I do keep my hands, and my suits, clean as much as possible. That, however, does not mean I haven't had to wash blood off both of them before."

Jeb spit at the ground. "From where I'm standing it looks like that blood come from folks much weaker than you. Coward."

The movement was a blur. Almost before Jeb could register it, Vanderheist had stepped forward, his fist coming down in an arc that busted Jeb's nose, blood immediately flowing freely across his lips and cheek. Stars danced across his vision as Jeb fell back and then was quickly righted by the arms supporting him.

As his vision cleared, Vanderheist was once again in his original position, just inches out of Jeb's reach. The man had pulled a handkerchief from his pocket and was inspecting his knuckles. He looked into Jeb's eyes for a moment and then spoke.

"I'm sure you have plenty to say now about how I struck a man who was held down, how I should let you free and we can settle things, etcetera, etcetera. So, if you don't mind, I'd like to go ahead and move beyond the tough words.

"I'm a businessman, Mr. Barnett. I don't make any money from big talk and I see no increase in my bank account by standing up for what is right, by putting my pride on the line. At the end of the day, one of us is going to be rich and one of us, if you keep yourself under some kind of control, might just not be a widower two times over. That's entirely up to you, though. The fact is, numbers don't lie. That's where my affinity for them comes from, in fact.

"Look around you, Jeb. There are five men here. There is one lawman. One scared wife. Two innocent children." Meeting Jeb's glare, the man grinned again. "I'm not a monster. I understand morals. I don't blame these children for anything. I have nothing against them. Where you and I differ, and I'm afraid you won't care for this one bit, but where you and I differ, Sheriff, is that I see their *intrinsic* value. You see a family. I see leverage.

"I must say, it's noble what you've done here. Some might wonder, though, given how you seem to have benefited from the demise of your previous deputy ..."

Jeb felt his anger getting the best of him. He clenched his jaw, welcoming the pain from where he'd been hit, willing it to keep him grounded.

Vanderheist smiled. "But those rumors don't need to get started. Folks will talk. New items of interest will arise. Believe it or not, I'm not here to ruin you, Mr. Barnett. Admittedly, the thought did cross my mind. My associate Trevor here" — he nodded to one of the men standing by Shae — "had actually come up with a very fine plan in which we simply came into your home and shot you where you lay. So, in a way, and as much as I'm sure it riles your chivalrous heart, you owe me a bit of a thanks. If I hadn't decided to come along this evening, well, you'd have a bullet in your brain right now. As for your family ..." Vanderheist shrugged, letting Jeb's mind fill in the blank. "So," the man folded his handkerchief and tucked it back in his breast pocket. "I'm waiting, Mr. Barnett."

Jeb looked over at Shae. The woman had tears running down her cheeks, but her back was straight, her eyes aflame. She shook her head once, firmly.

"I mean, we could revert to Plan A," Vanderheist said, opening his suit jacket to reveal the revolver strapped to his hip. "It's really not much concern to me. Slightly messier, perhaps. But, that's where planning pays off." He looked at Jeb. "Which will it be?"

Jeb stared back at the man, knowing he had no choice, knowing the bitter words would haunt him. But, with the taste of blood in his mouth, he forced himself to stand upright, look the man in the eyes.

"I thank you, Mr. Vanderheist," he said slowly.

The criminal smiled. "Now, was that so hard?"

"I thank you for giving me the chance to watch you hang."

Vanderheist laughed. "Wonderful," he said. "Just wonderful. I would expect no less from a real live cowboy." He turned to the men guarding Shae and made a gesture. "Unfortunately, we have other business to attend to and I must bring our meeting to a close. I assure you though, Sheriff, you'll be hearing from me soon. In the meantime, remember who is tending to your family. You control what kind of attention they will receive."

He turned and walked back to the group, calling over his shoulder, "Give the sheriff something to help him remember this."

The first fist connected with his temple, knocking him to the ground. Dazed, Jeb felt boots drive into his stomach, his back. Through the fog, he thought he could see his gun. If he could just crawl there …

A boot heel hit his thigh, the leg almost immediately numb. Another came down on his hand, grinding the bones together. Briefly, through a sheen of blood, he saw one of the men bending down to meet his eye.

"See ya soon, Sheriff," the man said.

Jeb vaguely registered the leg pulling back before the kick caught him on the side of the head and he blacked out.

Chapter Nineteen

Hands shook his shoulders. A wet cloth on his forehead. A voice.

Jeb groaned, brushing at the hand. He was outside, on the ground. The taste of blood brought him back to his senses. He started to sit up, letting out a slight moan at the pain. It was everywhere. He raised a hand to his forehead but the arm was weak, shaking. The sun shone down in his eyes and he winced away from it.

"Jeb," the voice said again. It was soft, feminine, but the undertone of urgency couldn't be mistaken. "Oh thank heavens, Jeb. I thought you were dead."

He allowed the hands to help him right himself. He felt about blindly, finding the hand with the cloth and directing it to his eyes. Crusted blood had sealed the left one shut. He wiped at the right with the handkerchief, his vision slowly clearing.

In front of him, on her knees, sat his neighbor Grace. "Jeb, what happened? Where's Shae and the kids?"

"Grace," he said, his voice gravelly, dusty in his throat. He coughed, spat on the ground. "Help me up."

The woman gave him a doubtful look but finally hooked his arm over her small shoulder. "You're gonna have to work at this too; I can't carry you all the way inside."

"No," he said. "Just up. I gotta go."

"You couldn't make it to the porch on your own. What're you talking about going any place? What happened here last night?"

"My gun," Jeb said, the world tilting and righting itself as he fought to regain his balance without losing consciousness again. "It's around."

"Yeah, yeah, your gun," the woman said. "I saw it over there. You can go two minutes without your gun. I ain't gonna hurt ya."

He shuffled along beside her, realizing they were headed toward the house. "No," he said. "I need to find Aaron. Get my gun."

The woman didn't respond. Instead, she continued to guide his stumbling body toward the porch, almost losing him as he fought her going up the steps, and then with a nudge of her hip, she deposited him in one of the rocking chairs.

She sighed, pushing the hair back off her forehead. "I'll get your gun, and I can find Aaron, but you need to do some talking first. Where is Shae?"

"I'll find her," Jeb said, rubbing his face with the hankie. "Wet this again." He gestured toward the rain barrel.

"Awfully bossy for a man just back from the dead," she said, taking the cloth and walking over to the rain barrel.

"Vanderheist," Jeb said finally. "Came last night. Took Shae and the kids." He reached out for the hankie and rubbed the water around his face and neck, thankfully feeling the fuzziness leave his mind as he went through the actions. He hurt. Everywhere. But he was alive. No bones seemed to be broken. He pawed at his left eye with the cloth, smearing away the blood and forcing it to open.

"I don't know no Vanderhamm," the woman said.

"Heist," Jeb said. "You be glad you don't." He paused for a moment, looking up at her. "Why are you here?"

"Your horse," she said, gesturing toward where the animal was tied to the front fence. "She was out having breakfast in our front yard."

"Thanks," he said.

"What's going on here, Jeb? I need answers and you need a doctor."

"No," he said. "No doctor. I ain't got time for that."

Grace started to reply but he held up a hand, cutting her off. "Listen," he said. "I'll fill you in some time, but that time ain't now. Right now, I need you to get back home to your husband. Spread the word. Everybody needs to keep their heads down till I can get this under control. Don't be out wandering around. Lock your doors. I don't think there's any danger for you all, but I didn't think there was in this house either."

"Jeb, what's going on?" The woman's voice had an element of pleading in it, barely covered by her concern.

"Things've gotten out of hand," he said, standing slowly. "It's time I take care of it."

Grace looked at him. He could see her resistance in her eyes. He could even understand it to an extent.

"I have to do this, Grace. No way around it. You get home and take care of your own. I need anything, you'll be the first to know."

The woman hesitated for a moment, then sighed. "Oh, Jeb," she said. "Being the sheriff's neighbor is supposed to be *safe*." He watched as she hurried out into the yard, plucking his revolver from the dirt. "You find that man," she said, handing him the gun.

Jeb checked the chambers and tucked it into his holster. "You count on that," he said, walking slowly out to his horse.

*****

At the same time Jeb was making his slow ride into town, Edward Vanderheist was celebrating the success of their visit to the sheriff's home. With Shae and the children safely locked away in the cellar at Vanderheist's temporary home, he brought Trevor and the other men who had joined them to the bunkhouse for a rare moment of goodwill and camaraderie.

"It couldn't have gone better, my boys," Vanderheist said, raising a shot glass to the men. "Now that we've captured the queen, the king has no choice but to do as we ask." He looked over at Trevor, a devilish grin on his face. "And you wanted to shoot the poor man."

Trevor raised his glass and smiled somewhat. "I didn't think it through, sir. Your plan was much better."

Vanderheist laughed. "To sycophants!"

The men, somewhat confused, toasted with him, bringing an even louder laugh from the German. "Some day I need to sit down and have a proper school for you all."

The men exchanged looks.

"Imagine," Vanderheist said, the sleepless night and alcohol going somewhat to his head. "If I could simply train some men. It wouldn't have to be many. Ten, half a dozen. With just that number of reliable, smart men, I could own everything on this side of the Mississippi."

Trevor opened his mouth to respond, but at Edward's glance merely reached out and began refilling the shot glasses. Edward looked around at the men, realizing what must've been going through their heads.

"But who needs school when you have a sheriff, am I right, boys?" he said, raising his glass again.

The men broke into smiles, the passing discomfort having been replaced with the usual routine of lifting glasses and the relief at seeing Vanderheist with a smile on his face for once. The man looked around at the group, considering his momentary lapse in judgment. They had to know they were expendable, but it probably did them no good to be reminded of the fact. He pulled up a chair to the table just as one of the guards from the house stepped into the room.

"Man here to see you, boss."

"Oh?" Vanderheist said, sitting down.

"Says he's got a problem with a shipment."

"Receiving or dealing out?" Vanderheist smiled.

"Don't know, sir. Ain't my place to ask."

"Good man," Vanderheist said. Then, looking around the room, "Fellows, drink up. Enjoy the rest of your day. Perhaps I shall return."

The men toasted him as he followed his guard up to the main house. The alcohol felt warm in his stomach and, mixed with the success of the evening, brought a smile to his face.

***

Inside, Alex Carpenter stood in the entryway, hat in his hands. The man had been the cause of absolutely no problems for Vanderheist so far. So much so that, if it weren't for such an exceptionally unexceptional working relationship, Vanderheist might've forgotten the man's name.

"Mr. Carpenter," he said, sitting down and gesturing to a chair nearby. "What brings you to my home this fine morning? Something about a shipment, I hear?"

"Well, yes, sir," the man said, sitting down on the edge of the seat as if worried his dusty jeans would tarnish the spectacularly clean home. "We been hearing some things of late and, well, folks is getting a little antsy about moving the product."

"And what product are we discussing, precisely?"

"For the most part the moonshine, sir. Them guns get bought up and tucked away without no problem at all. Hell, I don't even know if half the fellers remember they bought 'em. If you'll excuse my language."

Vanderheist waved a hand. "We're both men here. I can't say I'm terribly surprised. The moonshine tends to help the guns move and, as you pointed out, often makes for forgetful purchases. It's actually been rather a boon to business," he said, grinning. "Get enough moonshine in a man and you can sell him more guns than he'll ever need. Sometimes he'll buy the same one twice."

"Yes." Carpenter smiled back. "I may have noticed that a time or two myself."

"Good man," Vanderheist said.

"Problem is, word's getting around that the sheriff is cracking down on things. I hear he's been sniffing around more'n he oughtta and it's made folks twitchy about buying up anything they shouldn't be. Like you said, if you get the liquor in 'em first, it ain't no problem. But now they's shying away from they drink, it's slowing down everything."

Vanderheist stood up and beckoned to the man. "Mr. Carpenter, I appreciate your concerns. And I appreciate you bringing them to me so forthrightly. But" — he raised a finger — "I have something you might appreciate even more." With a slight wobble in his step, Vanderheist led Carpenter over to where one of his men stood guard at a door. With a quick gesture, Vanderheist shooed the guard away, unlocked the door with a key from his pocket, and ushered his business partner down into the cellar.

"I give you," Vanderheist said with a small bow, "the solution to all our problems."

He watched as Alex's eyes adjusted to the dim room, the man glancing about briefly before finally settling on the forms of Shae and her two children.

"Mrs. Tulley!" the man said.

Vanderheist burst into laughter. "How rude, sir! Mrs. Tulley no more! This is the new Mrs. Barnett. Surely you heard the news."

"Well, yes, sir. I just ..." Carpenter stumbled over his words. "I didn't expect this."

"It is quite the surprise, isn't it?" Vanderheist said, turning the man and leading him back to the stairs. "The beauty of it is, neither did the sheriff. So, as you can see, Jeb Barnett won't be sticking his nose anywhere it needn't be so long as we have the upper hand. You hurry back to where you came from and spread the word, Mr. Carpenter. The sheriff is mine."

Chapter Twenty

Jeb had just sat down in the temporary office when Aaron burst through the door. The deputy was breathing hard, dusty, and clearly hadn't been out of bed long.

"I came as fast as I could!" he panted out.

Jeb gestured to a chair. "Sit down," he said, wincing at the motion. "I was gonna come find you in a minute anyway. Word spread that fast, huh?"

Aaron sat down in the seat, leaning forward. "I don't know about that," he said. "Grace come and found me. Musta left your place and headed straight for mine. Jeb, I'm so sorry."

The sheriff looked down at his hands, rubbed at his bruised, most likely cracked, ribs. "You can be sorry later, though I don't know precisely what it is you got to be sorry for. I was the one they got the jump on. I was the one who lost his gun. I was the one who had to stand there and watch that man cart off my family. If you'da been there, most likely we'd be two dead bodies on my yard right now."

"At least we wouldn't be the only two," Aaron said.

"And what good would that do us?" Jeb asked. "Maybe we'd've got a couple of 'em, but that don't solve nothing for Shae and the kid. Look, I appreciate the fire in ya, but we can't be running out there and kicking down doors. We gotta do this smart. I think we may've underestimated this feller. This ain't no run-of-the-mill outlaw. The man's smart. He thinks ahead. And right now he's got us in a real situation."

Aaron grinned. "But just us."

Jeb looked at him, adjusting in the seat and wincing at the motion.

"The man's smart, okay, I'll give ya that," Aaron said. "But everybody makes mistakes. He thought he was being smart catchin' you unawares, coming in the middle of the night like that. Probably figured you'd be asleep, sure. But he also probably figured you'd be alone."

"Well, he figured right on that account," Jeb said.

"And now that he's been right once, he's probably gonna keep figuring on being right. Sure he might expect you to be a little more cautious, but I bet he's thinking you're outta moves now. Just you and me and what little help we can muster up. Shoot, even if we call in from outta town he'd hear about it before it done us any good. That sound about right?"

"Sounds about right cause it is about right. Least for the time being. What're you thinking?"

"Look," Aaron said, "we were gonna head out to the tribe today already, remember? Take Shae and the kids out there to keep 'em safe."

"Right."

"Well, I say we saddle up and get going. We may not have your family with us, but I think that might give us something even more important."

Jeb looked at the young man, feeling his enthusiasm grow to match Aaron's even if he didn't precisely understand the deputy's implications.

"Them Comanche don't care none for this Vanderheist, least not much more than any of the rest of us. We ride out there and let the chief know what happened, he'll make a move. I guarantee it."

"They keep to themselves though, Aaron. I don't know."

"Don't matter," Aaron said. "You're just talking about the why's. Maybe the chief wouldn't get involved if the reason was just to get Shae back. In fact, you're probably right. They draw the line, and it's a hard one. But you know what else we got now? Proof. We got proof that Vanderheist don't have no line he won't cross. If that feller'll come after the sheriff's wife and kids, well there ain't no reason at all to think he wouldn't do the same to some Indian folk."

Jeb sat for a moment, thinking. Then, slowly, he stood, reaching for his hat on the wall. "I sure hope you're right," he said, turning toward the door. "Long ride out that way and I ain't in top shape. Let's go."

***

In their usual meeting place, for once, Aaron was animated. The deputy paced back and forth, gesturing as he spoke. It wore out Jeb just to watch the man, but if he wasn't mistaken, he saw just a ghost of a smile on the lips of the chief, in spite of the dark nature of the tale the men had come to tell.

After a few minutes, the chief gestured to Aaron. "Sit, please. I understand. Save your energy."

Aaron looked between the chief and Jeb and then finally took a seat on the log underneath the overhanging tree branches.

"Your friend is right," the chief said after a pause, looking over to Jeb. "If this man is willing to take your family, he will have no qualms about doing the same or worse out here. You at least have value to him. You're a tool he can use." The man gestured around him, indicating the tribe in general. "We are just a nuisance in his eyes. Either we buy his goods and he prospers, or we don't and we are in his way. I had intended to move on if you didn't find a way to control this man. Now it looks as if moving on might not be the answer to any of our problems."

"You said you'd protect my family," Jeb said. "I know matters have changed, but they still need protecting. Aaron and I was talking though, and I think we may have an idea."

The chief thought for a moment and then gestured for him to continue.

"You told us you expected to see this feller at the beginning of the month. That's two days from now. You got any reason to believe he ain't going to keep that appointment?"

"He wants to trade with us, he must come to where we are. That has always been the understanding."

"All right, good," Jeb said. "Way I figure, we can make sure this meeting goes the way we want it to, not the way he's expecting. Aaron and me are gonna head back into town and see if we can't rustle up a little help on that end without causing too much noise. I'll be honest with you though, Chief, I don't know how much that's gonna be. Word'll have spread by now and I reckon most folks are gonna be making the safe choice and staying out of this."

"What your people do is none of our concern," the older man said. "Our people will fight to protect their families. When Vanderheist comes, whether you do or not, we will be prepared."

Jeb stood and extended a hand. "You're an honorable man," he said. "And I am as well. You'll see the two of us again in twenty-four hours."

The chief shook his hand and nodded. "We will be prepared."

Chapter Twenty-one

The following forty-eight hours were tiresome ones for Jeb. Despite his body trying to mend, despite clandestine meetings with Aaron and some of the more reliable men in town, despite the countless hours in the saddle, he still couldn't sleep at night. Knowing Shae and the kids were somewhere, worse, somewhere close, and yet he was unable to help them left the man with many thoughts and little comfort in the dark hours of the night.

Aaron had stayed the first evening with him, stretching out on the living room floor. It was largely a pointless move, both men were aware of it. Vanderheist had everything he needed to keep Jeb in line, at least as far as the outlaw was concerned. Lying in bed, Jeb wondered. If their plan fell apart somehow, Vanderheist would not only still have the upper hand, he might feel the urge to do something to prove to Jeb just who was running things. Everything needed to go off without a hitch or the situation would be worse than it already was.

On the ride back out to the Comanche territory, a measly three men joining Jeb and Aaron, the sheriff had mentioned his concerns, if only briefly, and only under the guise of explanation to the men with him. Aaron, hot-tempered as he could sometimes be, was now showing the other side of his nature, the one that, to Jeb, should've been the more frightening of the two. Aaron had two sides to his character. The one, fiery, quick to anger, had come from his father. The other, calm, calculating, controlled, had come from his time with the tribe. Jeb had seen plenty of the first traits in men. It was what started barroom brawls and kept his cells full. Usually, though, men like this were remorseful and did their best to keep it from happening again.

The other side, the one that waited, watched, and then pounced, that was what made Aaron and men like him so valuable on the side of the law and so dangerous on the other. Vanderheist was a man just like that. Jeb had suspected it since they first spoke with the chief, but now, having dealt with the man first hand, Jeb had no doubts. It was one reason that, despite the small size of their party, he felt confident in the outcome of their plan. Aaron was quiet most of the ride, which meant, Jeb knew, the deputy was running through scenarios in his mind. He was looking for problems, holes, errors in judgment. Overpreparation is what some might call it, but if things took a turn, Aaron would already have a contingency plan in mind.

Until they'd met with the chief, Jeb had left Aaron to his own thoughts. Even after, when they'd gone over the plan for the ambush, split into groups, settled on positions and signals, Aaron had had little to share. Once, twice maybe, he pointed to a place on the improvised map drawn in the dirt. Then it dawned on Jeb; Aaron had little to offer because the man who had taught him everything was now taking charge of their encounter. Jeb found himself growing quieter as well, beginning to stop asking questions and start simply taking directions. With these two minds on their side, he also began to feel much more confident.

And so, as the sun came up on the first day of the month, Jeb was hunkered down not far from camp. It was a delicate decision, one of the few times he'd wondered about the chief's plan. They were close enough to hear clearly over the flat land, and seeing the interaction wouldn't be difficult, though accurate shooting from such a distance would be risky.

Then again, ideally, there would be no need for shooting. The chief had said Vanderheist only brought a handful of men with him, not many more than Jeb and Aaron had brought with them. But in this type of instance, Jeb preferred overwhelming force to anything even slightly resembling a fair fight. The chief had promised to do his best in providing men, but, as he rightly said, the fewer men Vanderheist saw around the area, the more likely he would be to suspect something was amiss.

In the end, Jeb and Aaron had each taken a group of four men and moved to flanking positions on either side of the trail leading into camp. Communicating mostly through the flash of small pocket mirrors, they'd been able to arrange themselves in a delicate string, positioning men far enough apart to effectively close off any exit strategies without being spread too thin.

By the time the morning dew had been baked away by the sun, everyone was in position, and the men had nothing left to do but wait.

The rocky terrain did little to soothe Jeb's aching body as he waited in the sun, crouched down behind what little cover there was available out in the scrub. Thankfully, around midmorning, the tell-tale dust of approaching horses kicked up to the east. Jeb tucked the small mirror into his shirt pocket, hoping Aaron, and more so the other men, had noticed the dust and would lay low until the signal was given. The last thing he needed was someone inadvertently tipping their hand when things were so close.

Before long, Jeb could make out the riders. Vanderheist, in his gray suit, sat straight in his saddle, three men on either side of him. It wasn't ideal, but then again, Jeb thought, what was? The more men that were out here, the more they had to contend with. But the fewer men accounted for meant the more left behind. Jeb pulled his revolver from the holster and waited. He supposed the only way to deal with problems was as they presented themselves. Perhaps once they'd cut the head off the snake the whole thing would die.

From where he had hunkered down, Jeb was close enough to make out the conversation, but shouldn't draw much attention to himself. As the group of bootleggers approached, the chief and two of his trusted men came out to meet them at the edge of camp.

Vanderheist reined in his horse and looked down at the man for a moment, perhaps enjoying the cheap feeling of superiority the height gave him. After a moment though, the stoic face of the chief drew Vanderheist down out of the saddle.

"If you don't mind, I've got some business to attend to," Vanderheist said. "I regret to say these matters were arranged between myself and some of your compadres, so we don't have too terribly much need for more cooks in the kitchen, as it were."

The chief looked at him, silent. Jeb understood the plan, or at least as much of one as it could be when so many of the steps began with phrases like 'assuming …' and 'if …' But patience and surprise were both on their side. He could wait a few more minutes. If he had to.

"Here, things don't happen without my approval," the chief said, his eyes never wavering from Vanderheist's.

The bootlegger smiled. "Well, unfortunately, my friend. The times are changing. I'm sure you've seen it yourself. Probably part of the reason you keep moving west. And I can't say I blame you. These Americans …" Vanderheist grinned, looking back over his shoulder. "They can be a tiresome lot." The men laughed. "But I must give them this, they are stubborn. As you've seen, the farther west you go, the farther west they come. If it were up to me, I wouldn't be here bothering you. But, the times, well, they require it."

"You may go," the chief said.

Vanderheist smiled at him. "I may, I may. That's awfully kind of you to give me permission. But one of the things that is changing is that I don't particularly need your permission. You may be chief here. In fact, it looks like you have plenty of folks who are willing to treat you just that way. But the fact is, they don't have to. And not all of them do. Now, some of your folks and my boys here, well, we've got some things to discuss and I'd be much obliged if you'd step aside and allow us to conduct our business."

The chief made no movement, but the two men on his sides both stepped forward.

Vanderheist laughed quietly. "I guess the Americans aren't the only stubborn ones out here, are they? The problem here, Chief, isn't whether or not I like you or you like me. It isn't about whether you approve of how I do business or not. In fact, it really doesn't have much to do with anything except one cold, hard fact." He gestured to the men behind him, who then dismounted and formed a ring around their leader. "There are more of us than there are of you."

The chief paused for a moment, just long enough to let Vanderheist think he had the upper hand, then called out one phrase in the tribe's language.

"*Suhmuh nokimaruh.*" Come, all of you.

They were the words Jeb had been waiting to hear. He glanced only briefly to the right and left, seeing his men leap forth from their hiding positions on one side of the trail, Aaron and his men doing the same across from them. But even this movement was lost in the blur of motion from the tribe. Almost as if from nowhere, men materialized around the chief, seeming to appear from the shadows, the insides of teepees, practically from the ground itself.

Jeb raced across the short distance, his eyes on the men around Vanderheist, the boss himself suddenly obscured from view as his gang of outlaws closed in around him. The man closest to Jeb went for his gun, a fatal mistake. Before the barrel could clear the holster Jeb had fired, bringing the man down.

Startled, a few of the men, including Vanderheist, turned to the sound of the gunshot. At the sight of Jeb and his men rushing toward them, there was a moment of confusion, some turned the other way, only to find themselves staring down Aaron and his posse. One reached for the pommel on his saddle, a last-ditch effort to make some kind of move toward escape, but before he could mount, even Vanderheist saw the futility of the action.

"Come down," Jeb heard Vanderheist bark at the man. "Act as if you've got at least a modicum of sense about you. Surely you don't plan to outride bullets today."

"You sure you don't wanna give it a try?" Jeb said, grabbing Vanderheist by the collar.

"Ah, Mr. Barnett, I should've assumed I'd find you out here somewhere," the man said. "I must say, well played. Though I must wonder, if all your men are out here, what do you suppose is happening in your town?"

"Nice try," Jeb said, fastening the man's hands behind his back. "You just can't admit when you're whipped, can you?"

Vanderheist smiled. "I find there are usually more outcomes than one initially plans on."

"Y'know, there you're right. I just about bet you didn't plan on leading me back to my family today, did ya?" Jeb turned the man around and led him to a horse, helping him climb up into the saddle. "Today's just fulla surprises."

Vanderheist looked down from the saddle and laughed. "Today, yes. Tomorrow, as well, I'm sure."

Jeb turned back to Aaron. "You handle the rest of 'em," he paused. "Unless, chief, you got anything you want taken care of first?"

The faint grin passed across the man's lips again. "Go," he said, simply.

Chapter Twenty-two

In the courthouse a few days later, Jeb sat with Aaron and the county judge, a book on the table between them. Vanderheist's trial had been fast and smooth, perhaps yet another surprise the man hadn't been counting on. Once word spread of his arrest, his previously loyal men had scattered to the wind. Even the man who had opened the door to the cellar for Jeb had been gone by the time he and Vanderheist had resurfaced — the latter with a stinging red palm mark across his cheek.

Jeb had sent Shae and the kids home that day, escorted Vanderheist to the makeshift prison that had been erected since the fire, and personally sat guard until Aaron and the other men had returned with the rest of the posse. Walking out, he'd taken a moment to shake each man's hand, hearing variations of "oh it's nothing," and "we didn't do much," as he made his way down the line. At the door, he'd paused.

"Maybe you fellers don't think you did much, since you didn't have to fire them guns hanging at your hips. But what I seen was three men who didn't have no business putting their life on the line other'n they thought it was the right thing to do. When we rode out you didn't know what to expect. I'm thankful we all come back in one piece and are able to say it 'warn't nothing.' I owe you men more than I can say. Any of you ever need anything, you know where to find me." He paused on the threshold of the door and turned back. "I may need one more favor of ya, though."

Smiles met his grin.

"I'm plumb tuckered out, and despite what he says, ole Aaron here could use a bit of a rest his own self. These boys ain't going nowhere less you hand 'em the keys. How y'all feel about bein' deputized?"

One of the men laughed. "Just like that, huh?"

"Just like that," Jeb smiled. "I am the sheriff around here, after all. We can celebrate later. For now, I'm off to see my wife."

The reunion had been sweet, heartfelt, full of tears. Both from happiness and from other, more deep-set, harder to express emotions. Part of it had been anger. Not with one another, but at the audacity of a man to act as Vanderheist had done. Part had been relief, the letting go of all the pent-up emotions both Shae and Jeb had held inside, wanting to stay strong, wanting to believe justice would prevail, not wanting to consider any other outcome. In the end, the family had fallen asleep together in the front room. Jeb woke around midnight, leaning over to kiss Shae on the head before they took the children up to their beds and retired to the main bedroom themselves.

And it had been good, all of it. But it left a few threads dangling. One had been the trial of Edward Vanderheist and his men. While it had been simple enough to bring him in, discerning and specifying the vast amount of charges against the man had taken time. In the end, the judges and lawyers had come to an agreement that would send the man away for a very long time. Despite Vanderheist's assurances that he'd be back sooner than they expected.

"You come on back anytime," Aaron had called as the man had been escorted from the courtroom. "We'll round you up as many times as you want."

Which left them with the book on the table between them. Richard's diary. Jeb had kept the book away from Shae, not even letting her know of its existence. While it had been valuable in the trial as proof of Vanderheist's liquor and gun business, the man's own books had been more than enough to tie him to numerous illegal activities, not only in Texas but up through Oklahoma and as far east as Missouri as well.

Now that the trial was over, the question was what were they to do with it?

The judge placed his hand on the worn cover of the book, looking over at Jeb. "As far as I'm concerned, this book need not exist. The charges have been laid, the man has been convicted. What's laying here now is merely page after page of heartache for a woman who's already seen enough of that for one lifetime."

Jeb nodded, looking over at Aaron.

"I'd burn it for you right now if you want me to," the deputy said. "Richard had us all fooled. I ain't proud of it, but I also don't see no sense in dragging a man's name through the mud when he ain't here to defend himself. Whatever he done, he had his reasons. Maybe I wouldn't agree with them, but there's no changing it now. And you ask me, he more than paid for his mistakes."

Jeb looked up to the judge again.

"As I said from the bench," the judge said. "As far as myself, the county, and anyone who wants to know, this case is closed. Burn it, throw it down a well, but I agree with your friend. There's nothing more to be done in the matter."

Jeb stood up, taking the book and holding it in front of him for a moment. It was so many things. Evidence of crime. Evidence of betrayed friendships. Of a broken marriage. The greed of a man who had paid with his life.

And also, it was just the worn-out notebook of a man who'd rolled the dice and lost.

Jeb tossed it back on the table. "I reckon y'all can do what you will with it then. Ain't got no use for me."

He settled his hat on his head, turned, and walked out of the room.

Epilogue

Shae stood at the window in the kitchen, her hands resting on the cutting board. Outside, Grace held Daisy while Ben ran amuck in the sideyard, caught up in some kind of imaginary game Shae could only guess at. As usual, Ben had bounced back from their incident with a resilience she could only envy. Outside of asking to sleep in their bed the first night or two, he'd been a typical boy and run himself so ragged during the daytime that he could often barely keep his eyes open through dinner.

"He's a tough boy," Jeb had said.

"Like his father," she'd replied.

A pause had hung in the air as both considered the words she'd uttered.

Finally, Jeb said, "He was a good man."

Shae had flushed then, realizing Jeb had interpreted the comment in just the way she'd thought, though not in the way she'd hoped. "Richard was a lot of things," she'd said, looking at Jeb over the dinner table. "Maybe we saw different sides of him. But who he was doesn't matter now. When I said that, Jeb, I meant you."

The man had looked down at his plate then, nodding a little. It was always his way when things became too emotional. But she knew this about him and it spoke to her in ways his words might not have been able to. This was the man she loved, no matter what winding path had brought them together, she knew this was where she belonged.

As if on cue, and bringing Shae out of her revelry, she heard Ben cry out in the yard.

"You're home!"

She watched as the boy raced across to the man, his arms extended, leaping up toward the sheriff without even the slightest doubt that he would be caught.

Jeb flipped the boy up over his shoulder, taking off his hat and waving to Grace. "May as well come in and join us. I reckon you earned a meal or two lately."

The woman laughed. "I've got my own hungry boys at home, sheriff. I can't be over here tending to you all hours of the day and night. You're still limping, I see."

Jeb stopped, twisting Ben around so the boy fell into his arms. "You hear that?" he said in a mock whisper. "You think I been limping?"

The boy grinned up at him.

"Oh, I see," Jeb said. "You're all ganging up on me. Well, I got ways a dealin' with the likes of you!" He lifted Ben up by the ankles, dangling the laughing child in front of him as he took long steps toward the house. "You see any limpin'? I feel like maybe I just might break into a dance!"

"Noooo," Ben laughed, fighting with the shirt that kept attempting to fall into his eyes. "You don't dance! I dance!"

"You dance?" Jeb said, flipping the boy upright and setting him on his feet. "Well, now that's something I'd like to see."

"Watch!"

As Ben worked himself into a frenzy on the porch, Shae stepped into the doorway behind him, a hand cupped to her mouth, laughter bringing tears to her eyes.

"Well, I'll be," Jeb said, looking up at her. "We got us a dancing fool on our hands. Only one thing to do about that."

"Jebediah, don't you dare!"

In a bound, Jeb was on the porch, his arms around Shae's waist.

"What're you gonna do?" Ben asked, still shuffling his feet beside them.

"Well, we're gonna join you, a'course!"

As Grace clapped a rhythm, taking Daisy's small hands in her own, Jeb twirled his bride along the wooden planks, reaching down to take the hand of his son, and felt truly, finally, home.

Extended Epilogue

About a year later, a very pregnant Shae sat at one end of the dining room table, Jeb at the other. Ben and Daisy had their own side, the girl in a high chair Jeb had built out in the barn specifically for her. Of course, not one to be left out, Ben had quickly requested a chair of his own, and Jeb had done his best to match the childish drawing of a throne while still keeping it under control enough that Shae would actually allow it in the house.

In the end, a deal had been struck for special occasions, something Ben had been quick to take advantage of. So, on this particular day, given that Aaron was joining them for dinner and Aaron didn't join them every single night for dinner, Ben sat proudly on his throne. Try as he might, Ben had yet to convince his parents that the presence of Alice, the new maid, constituted a special occasion.

"She's here every evening," Shae had explained.

"But she's still special," Ben had said, winning the argument for a few nights a week.

Jeb looked over at Aaron, watching the man's eyes follow the maid around the room. Ben clearly wasn't the only one who thought Alice was special. Jeb had mentioned it to the deputy more than once, but it turned out that Aaron's quiet side didn't only come out in moments of stress. The man had simply smiled and quickly changed the subject.

"Aaron," Ben had called from his majestic seat. "Do you wanna come over tomorrow?"

Feigning ignorance, the man looked up at the ceiling. "Hm ... I don't know. Seems like I have something important to do tomorrow. Now ... What was that? Do you remember?"

"It's my birthday!" Ben had stood up. "We're having a party! You have to come! Mom and Dad and me and Daisy." He rolled his eyes slightly. "And Alice and you!"

"And Grace?" Shae asked.

"Yeah, her too! And the other deputies! Everybody!"

Aaron laughed. "That's a heck of a party you're planning. But hey, I have a question. Who's gonna be running the town if all the deputies and your pa are here?"

Ben thought for a moment and then grinned mischievously. "Nobody!"

"Whoa now," Aaron said. "I don't know about that. How about we keep one or two fellers at the office? They can take turns."

"Okay!" Ben plopped back down in his seat and resumed eating, all pressing issues, to his mind, resolved.

"You won't be taking a turn though, will you?" Shae asked.

Aaron looked over at Jeb and grinned. "I don't think she's askin' me, boss."

Jeb grinned and shook his head. "You've more than earned the right to make your own schedule. As for me, there's only one place I'm gonna be tomorrow."

"Less the place burns down again?"

"Well," Jeb smiled. "You've dealt with that before. I'll be here when y'all need me. But from here on out, this is where I belong. Besides" — he raised an eyebrow — "I don't plan on being sheriff forever."

The deputy's mouth dropped open.

"We'll talk about it later," Jeb said. "I'm sure you'll wanna have all the details before you go spreading the word. Besides, I'm kinda thinking I got everything I want in life right here. Maybe I'll just enjoy it for a while."

THE END

Also by Zachary McCrae

Thank you for reading **"The Inevitable Hunt"**!

If you liked this book, you can also check out **my full Amazon Book Catalogue at:**
https://go.zacharymccrae.com/bc-authorpage

Thank you!